Feel the Bern

Copyright © 2022 by Andrew Shaffer

All rights reserved.
Published in the United States by Ten Speed Press, an imprint of Random House, a division of Penguin Random House LLC, New York.
TenSpeed.com
RandomHouseBooks.com

Ten Speed Press and the Ten Speed Press colophon are registered trademarks of Penguin Random House LLC.

Snowflake illustration on page 209 © 123levit - stock.adobe.com

Typefaces: Melvastype's Buinton Rough, Zetafonts's Cocogoose, Adobe Font's Warnock Pro

Library of Congress Cataloging-in-Publication Data is on file with the publisher.

Trade Paperback ISBN: 978-1-9848-6114-6
eBook ISBN: 978-1-9848-6115-3

Printed in USA

Acquiring editor: Matt Inman | Production editor: Ashley Pierce |
    Editorial assistant: Fariza Hawke
Front cover designer: Vi-An Nguyen | Designer: Annie Marino |
    Production designer: Mari Gill
Production manager: Dan Myers
Copyeditor: Michael Fedison | Proofreader: Christine Jerome
Publicists: David Hawk and Melissa Folds | Marketers: Joseph Lozada
    and Allison Renzulli

1st Printing

First Edition

Also by Andrew Shaffer

FICTION

Fifty Shames of Earl Grey

The Day of the Donald

Catsby: A Parody

Hope Never Dies

Hope Rides Again

Secret Santa

NONFICTION

Great Philosophers Who Failed at Love

Literary Rogues

How to Survive a Sharknado and
Other Unnatural Disasters

Ghosts from Our Past

Ain't Got Time to Bleed

POETRY

Look Mom I'm a Poet (And So Is My Cat)

Feel the Bern

"What happens in Vermont, stays in Vermont. But not much ever happens."

TRADITIONAL VERMONT SAYING

Chapter 1

Every Vermonter has a Bernie Sanders story.

This is mine.

It begins when I was in elementary school. Bernie was visiting our classroom to warn us of the coming climate catastrophe. Heavy stuff for a seven-year-old girl. "Let me be clear," he said in that gravelly baritone of his, "the future of the planet is in your hands. Now is not the time for thinking small."

I glanced over at the sleepy-eyed boy next to me who was spooning paste from a jar into his cakehole like it was a pint of Ben & Jerry's. If the future depended on kids like Brandon, the planet was screwed. Luckily for Mother Nature, I made a silent but solemn vow to pick up the slack. I could already tell that life was going to be just another group project, one where I would be stuck doing most of the work.

Years would pass before I could let Bernie know how much his visit influenced my decision to go into politics. By the time I volunteered on his presidential campaigns, he'd become a big deal. Suddenly, everybody wanted to "feel the Bern." It wasn't until grad school that I found myself in the same room with him again.

At twenty-three, I was one of the younger students in Georgetown's poli-sci program. Second-year students are required to complete a semester-long congressional internship, and the Sanders office was at the top of my list. And not just for the home-state connection. Unlike most internships in town, Bernie's actually paid a living wage. If I got into the program, I could take a much-needed break from Lincoln's Chinstrap, the DC dive I bartended at part-time. Playing therapist for sloshed, emotionally wounded older men is less fun than it sounds.

Some congressional offices swiped right on anyone with a pulse. Not the Sanders office. Everyone I knew in my grad program was applying there, even the lone Young Republican (bless his tiny bow tie). With such a large applicant pool, Bernie could afford to be selective. Only the best of the best made it into the program; only the best of the best of the best made it through the program. It was said that if you could survive a semester interning in the Sanders office, you could survive anything—even a Cancún vacation with Ted Cruz. Prospective employers knew this. A letter of recommendation from his office could get your foot in any door in town . . . except for the Sanders office, ironically. Bernie already had his ride-or-die squad. The chances of getting a full-time job with him after the internship were about as good as the chances of Elon Musk getting to Mars.

When I learned that I'd secured an in-person interview with the senator, I thought, *Of course I did.* Not to brag, but my CV game was strong: Dean's List, Honor Roll, you name it. Grades had never been a problem for me. Still, this town was stacked with straight-A students (excluding members of Congress, of course).

Now that I'd made the cut, I needed to do something to distance myself from the pack. Something bold. Something that would make Bernie remember the name "Crash Robertson." And not just because I was the only girl named "Crash" on the planet. Like Alexander Hamilton, I needed to shoot my shot.

As luck would have it, I knew Bernie's one and only weakness.

Most people think he's nothing more than a political machine, a man whose only hobby is fighting for the working class. While there's some truth to that, even political machines need fuel. A little birdie told me on good authority that the senator was a sucker for Vermont maple syrup. The little birdie was my mother, who managed the general store back in my hometown of Eagle Creek, Vermont ("New England's #1 Leaf-Peeping Destination!" according to a press release put out by the Eagle Creek Chamber of Commerce).

Grade A Golden, my mother texted me. *The lighter the better.*

She also asked if I would invite Bernie to be the grand marshal of our town's harvest festival parade. Outside of maple syrup, Champ Days is, like, the one thing people in my hometown are proud of. It's all so cringe. *Let me get the job first*, I'd texted back.

Okay, so Alexander Hamilton never thanked anyone for their time with a bottle of syrup. Nobody quashes political beef with duels anymore, either. They just duke it out on Twitter.

Bernie's chief of staff met me in the waiting area of the Sanders office. It was a typically sauna-like afternoon in mid-August and Lana O'Malley was dressed head-to-toe in black. Either she was immune to the heat, or she actually enjoyed it.

Lana ushered me into a windowless conference room without a word. Bernie, seated at the table in a rumpled baby-blue button-down shirt, looked like he'd just been roused from a nap. He might well have been—the Senate was in summer recess, and Bernie was still in DC interviewing a parade of fanboys.

He reached across the table to shake my hand. "Bernie Sanders," he said with that famously gruff voice, the one that made him sound like he was on a Brooklyn street corner hawking newspapers announcing an end to the Great War.

"Crash Robertson," I said, shaking his hand. As I was taking a seat, I spied half a dozen bottles of syrup pushed to the far end of the table, all presumably left behind by my competition. My heart sank. The half-pint of artisanal syrup in my handbag had cost me a week's worth of tips at Lincoln's Chinstrap. If I didn't get the internship, I would be eating ramen for the next month. And not the good stuff from the food trucks near campus.

"You want to be a campaign manager," Lana said, reading off my application.

"I volunteered on both of the senator's presidential campaigns," I said. "The energy was off the charts. There's something about being in a room with so many people, all working toward one goal. It all seems so unpredictable and exciting and amazing and now I'm rambling, aren't I?"

"Take a breath, you're fine," Lana said. "To be clear, though, this internship is a desk job. We don't have campaign staff at the moment. The senator has a few years before he's up for reelection."

"Don't remind me," Bernie mumbled.

What I was after was experience, I told Lana. A chance to learn the ropes from the best of the best. "I've heard this office is where coal is turned into diamonds," I said.

Bernie's frown deepened. "We support clean energy here."

Throughout the rest of the interview—correction: *interrogation*—I kept waiting for Bernie to jump in with a question of his own. Even mentioning how inspirational his elementary school visit had been failed to get a reaction out of him.

My ten minutes flew by. Either that, or Lana was showing me mercy by cutting the interview short. There were more victims waiting in the lobby. "Do you have any questions for us?" she asked absently, scrolling through messages on her Apple Watch.

I was ready to take the loss when my eyes fell again on the cluster of maple syrup bottles. Several were corporate brands cut with cheap corn syrup, easily distinguishable by their garish labels and faux-homestyle names such as "Maplewood Springs" and "Canadian Gold." Someone had even brought Bernie an old bottle of Aunt Jemima's, which had been discontinued when Quaker Oats realized nobody wanted their pancakes with a side of racism. The bottles lined up in a row all had one thing in common, though: they were all as dark and thick as used motor oil. There wasn't a single bottle of light syrup on the table.

Screw it. I reached into my handbag for my bottle. As I whipped it out, Lana reached out to intercept it like a Secret Service agent throwing herself in front of the president.

Bernie muscled it away from her. "Doc McGilliam's Barrel-Aged Golden Reserve Batch," he said, reading the label in quiet reverence. "Holy moly."

Mom had said I couldn't go wrong with Doc's. He was a local eccentric who produced some of the finest artisanal syrup in the state. The only trouble was finding it. It had been a tough season for sugarmakers in Vermont. Another abnormally warm spring. The early harvest—the source of all light, golden-hued syrup—had been hit the hardest. Stores had sold out of what little was produced months ago. Thankfully, that's why they'd invented the internet.

"This is impossible to find right now," Bernie continued, reading over the label. "Tastes like honey. In fact, I was bidding on a bottle of this just last week. Some jerk kept driving up the price . . ."

His eyes narrowed. I could practically see the gears spinning in his head. He was dangerously close to unmasking ruthless eBayer "Crash Bandi-loot" as the twenty-three-year-old across the table from him. In the closing minutes of the auction, I'd lobbed bids like hand grenades at my rival, "bernardsanders2016." I thought I'd been in a heated back-and-forth with a fellow Sanders supporter, not the man himself.

"Doc's from my hometown," I said, fumbling to cover my tracks. "He and my mom are old friends. She runs the general store up in Eagle Creek. The Vermont Country Shed. Perhaps you've driven past? You can't miss the American flag out front."

"It's the size of a drive-in movie screen," he said, spreading his arms wide. "Speaking of huge, I heard a rumor that some private tech company is buying up maple farms around Eagle Creek. They're talking about 'disrupting' the syrup industry."

"I haven't been back in a while," I said. "But it would be a shame to see the maple syrup industry go the way of every other industry in this country. I don't see that happening, though. Not in Eagle Creek. We were 'buy local' before it was a thing. There isn't a chain store or fast-food restaurant in sight."

"You all still have that harvest festival? It used to be a huuuge deal."

"It still is," I said. "At least in Eagle Creek. They're looking for a grand marshal for the parade. If you know anyone who might be interested in that sort of thing . . ."

Lana snatched the Doc McGilliam's from Bernie and set it off to the side with the other bottles. "While I'm sure the senator would love to hear more, I'm afraid our time is up. Now if you'll excuse us . . ."

"I had one more question, Lana, if you don't mind," Bernie said. He turned to me. "When can you start?"

Chapter 2

The prehistoric corded phone at the front desk was ringing again. There wasn't any caller ID on it, meaning there was
no way to know who was waiting for you when you picked up.
Normally, the office assistant would have answered before the
second ring. Cheylene had taken the day off, however, as had
practically everyone else in the office. I'd volunteered to sit at
the front desk, believing that—with nobody else around—there
would be plenty of downtime to study. And when I'd arrived at
eight thirty Thursday morning, the Hill was indeed a ghost town.
Unfortunately, Bernie's constituents hadn't gotten the memo that
the long weekend had unofficially started early. Hence the phone's
incessant yapping.

To be fair to the callers, it wasn't their fault for interrupting
my study time. The holiday coming up on Monday was Columbus
Day. Hardly a major holiday. The only people who even observed
it anymore were over retirement age (i.e., Congress). More and
more states were switching up the day to honor Native Americans

and Indigenous Peoples. In Eagle Creek, Columbus Day weekend had long been reserved for the harvest festival. Champ Days didn't have any connection to Christopher Columbus. Instead, it had started as a tongue-in-cheek celebration of Champ, Vermont's homegrown version of the Loch Ness Monster.

As I finally reached the phone, it went silent. I exhaled. When would these people learn this wasn't the twentieth century any longer? Unless your house is actively on fire, send an email. Or, better yet, just text like a normal person.

Other than my paralyzing fear of answering corded phones, working the front desk was mostly a breeze. Signing for deliveries? No big deal. Even the constituents who showed up hoping to speak to the senator didn't bother me—security stopped the real weirdos from making it to the office. Any weirdo who made it this far had an appointment. I'd only just returned to my textbook when the phone line lit up again.

"Senator Sanders's office," I answered, cradling the phone between my ear and shoulder.

"What's your favorite scary movie?" a distorted voice said.

Another *Scream* fan. Second one of the day. Prank calls were tired and dated when I was younger, but thanks to TikTok they were once again in vogue. I could hear the caller giggling. We were supposed to hang up on calls like this, but I decided to let off some steam.

"*Wolf of Wall Street*," I said.

There was a short pause before the caller said, "That's not a scary movie."

"Au contraire," I said. "Do you know how little has changed since the 2008 financial crisis? Wall Street is back to its old tricks. In some ways, the financial sector is more out of control than ever. Inequality in this country is rising at an all-time high—"

The line went dead. Good thing I was the only one in the office today. Why had I popped off like that? I blamed the weather. It was a gorgeous fall day in DC, seventy-two degrees without a cloud in sight. The trees were ablaze with color. I wanted to visit a pumpkin patch and eat apple cider donuts. What I didn't want to do was stare at a blank white wall. I'd known the internship would be an office gig, but how I envied all the campaign workers out there on the road. *Someday*, I told myself. *Someday.*

My phone buzzed in my handbag. I peeked to see who was texting.

It was my mother. *Tell Bernie THANK YOU for me!!!! You're the best XO XO XO.*

I responded with a GIF of a confused husky surrounded by question marks. What was I supposed to thank him for? Whatever she was going on about, it wasn't like I could just tap him on the shoulder and let him know my mom wanted to say hi.

This wasn't the first time she'd assumed I was literally working side by side with Bernie. To be fair, I hadn't done much to correct her. It was better for her to imagine me living my best life. Because reality? Let's say I'm not always a fan of it. If I wasn't filling in for Cheylene at the front desk, I was making photocopies or responding to constituent emails with form letters. Nothing earthshaking. The truth was that I had barely spoken to Bernie since getting hired. When he wasn't getting cantankerous on the Senate floor, he was on the road stumping for local progressive candidates across the country.

When I glanced up from my phone, Lana O'Malley was towering over me. I thought I'd sensed a dark cloud hovering. She was biting her thumb, something I'd noticed her doing when thinking something over. A deliberating technique. Or maybe she just liked the taste of her strawberry hand moisturizer.

"We have an issue," she said.

Bernie's chief of staff still hadn't warmed to me after that chilly interview. She was the lone gateway to the senator. If it was up to her—and it was—I wouldn't be getting a letter of recommendation out of the internship. In fact, she'd made it clear on more than one occasion I was lucky not to be shown the door early. Whenever I committed some arcane congressional intern faux pas, she was there to call me out. Yet by every objective metric, I'd outperformed the other interns by a country mile. Sure, I was crap at answering phones. But try to find anyone under thirty who didn't experience existential dread when faced with talking to a stranger on the phone. If Lana had heard me lose it on that last prank caller, though—

"What's the issue? Climate change? Inflation? Women's rights?"

"Food poisoning."

"Do I need to call the FDA?"

She sighed heavily. "Food poisoning in the district office," she said slowly as if I were a child, one she didn't like. "If you order the crab-stuffed lobster special at someplace called the 'Appaloosan Country Buffet,' you're accepting a certain level of risk. All we really need is one person this weekend—"

The phone began ringing, interrupting her. We both ignored it.

"Anyway," she continued, "Vermont's not a big place, and this weekend's schedule was all put together last minute. The senator was supposed to be taking it easy with his family in Burlington, but work calls, I suppose. I'd be surprised if any of his events draw more than fifty people. I would do it if I could, but I've got a wedding in Indiana this weekend. Who gets married in Indiana? Honestly."

"Hoosiers?"

She looked down at the ringing phone with a frown. "Are you going to answer that?"

I asked the caller to hold, then turned back to Lana.

"As I was saying," she continued, "asking interns to travel isn't standard operating procedure. But I thought, *Isn't Crash from Vermont?* This would be a great opportunity for a student, I would think. If you really want to see how the sausage gets made."

"Would I have to drive? My car is in the shop."

A lie. I hadn't had a car since high school.

"You'd be taking Amtrak," she said. "I'll make sure a driver is waiting for you at the train station in Burlington. It's a fairly light schedule. He's got a meet-and-greet, a picnic, a parade, and that's it. Some podunk harvest festival. Champion Days? No . . ."

"Champ Days?"

"That's it!" she said. "Have you been?"

I'd completely forgotten I'd mentioned the festival to Bernie. That explained my mother's text. Lana must have been calling around all morning looking for someone willing to give up their holiday weekend for a trip to rural Vermont. This wasn't a flashy Burlington event. To most of the staff, this was a bingo hall in a one-stoplight town. Joke was on them, though: Eagle Creek didn't have a bingo hall *or* a stoplight.

"I grew up going to Champ Days," I told Lana. "I've still got family in the area."

"Wait. It's coming back to me now. This is your hometown, isn't it?"

"Guilty as charged."

"And if I'm remembering correctly, you told us you hadn't been back home in some time. Is family going to be a problem?"

It had been a while since I'd been back to Eagle Creek. And by "a while," I mean "close to five years." I was your classic straight-A student, C-minus daughter. I'd been a little busy with school, obviously. (See: the Dean's List.) My mother had visited me in DC several times. She never asked when I was moving back. We both knew the answer.

No, I told Lana. Family shouldn't be a problem. And even if it was, how could I turn down one-on-one time with the senator?

"Well, I would . . . appreciate it," she said, which must have been hard for her. "It won't be too much for you, all by yourself?"

"I've brought way worse guys home to meet my mother," I joked.

"I was talking about the boss. You'll need to keep an eye on him, make sure he sticks to his schedule. He loves the outdoors. Can't stand to be cooped up. Any chance he gets, he'll try to 'get some fresh air.' He'll be due on stage in five minutes, and meanwhile he's in a rowboat on Lake Champlain asking local fishermen if they're registered to vote."

"If he tries to run, I'm pretty sure I can catch him," I said. "I run a quick 5K every morning."

"You shower afterward, right?" She sniffed the air around me. "What's your time?"

"For my daily run? Thirteen minutes a mile. In a race, under ten."

Lana nodded. "You might be okay. Depends how much of a head start he gets. He's got endurance—he was a distance runner in high school. Co-captain of his team. You've read his books. Doesn't run anymore, but he can move those legs faster than you might think."

"It sounds like you're asking me to babysit him."

"This isn't the Babysitter's Club, Crash. The senator is as sharp as ever. He isn't loosing it like . . . well, I won't say his name. Think of this more like 'Bernie Club.' The first rule of Bernie Club is: Don't let him out of your sight. Ever. I mean that literally. The second rule of Bernie Club is—"

"—really, *really* don't let him out of my sight, ever?"

"You got it," she said with a beaming smile. It was the sort of look you give your dog when it rolls over on command for the first time without a treat. Maybe that letter of recommendation was within reach, after all. Heck, I could even write it for her. I'd written plenty of my own progress reports over the years—it saved teachers time, and I like to think it showed initiative. This was my chance to prove to her I belonged in this office. All I had to do was keep Bernie Sanders safe and on schedule this weekend. In sleepy Eagle Creek. How hard could that be?

Chapter 3

The next night, my train pulled into Burlington. I lugged my clam-shell suitcase through the station in a zigzag pattern toward the escalator. One of my suitcase's wheels had broken in the train's overhead bin. It kept trying to turn me back toward the tracks. Did it know something about this trip that I didn't? *It's not an omen,* I told myself. Sometimes a cheap suitcase is just a cheap suitcase.

Twelve hours on a train wasn't something I ever wanted to do again. It would have taken half that without all the stopping and starting. I understood why the office booked staffers on trains when possible—commercial airplanes were notorious emissions offenders. On a positive note, I'd had plenty of time to work on that letter of recommendation. It was coming along nicely. Six handwritten pages in my notebook and pretty good so far. Just needed another synonym for "incomparable." *Outstanding? Primo? Unsurpassed on all fronts?*

I'd been told a car would be waiting for me out front. Eagle Creek was quite a hike from Burlington, so this was supposed to be a private car, not a ride-share. I imagined a black Cadillac and a sharp-dressed, debonair gentleman holding a sign with my name on it. Would he open the door for me with his white gloves? Would there be full-sized Fuji water bottles and hemp-seed granola bars waiting for me? Would I be able to control the air-conditioning from the back seat? I felt like Cinderella on her way to the ball.

And then I saw my prince.

Bernie Sanders.

He was standing by himself near the exit, holding a sheet of printer paper with my name Sharpied onto it.

"Senator," I said, trying to hide the shock in my voice and hastily stuffing my manifesto of recommendation into my handbag.

"Any other luggage?" he asked quickly. The rest of the passengers from my train were dispersing around the parking lot, oblivious to the senator in their midst. Bernie was dressed down in khakis and a light blue polo. A few tufts of white hair were poking out below his Brooklyn Dodgers dad cap. It was the state uniform for White Men of a Certain Age. No wonder nobody had recognized him.

I told him I'd only brought the one suitcase.

"Great," he said. "We need to get on the road before they tow me. I'm parked in the Uber lane."

I followed him to his car, a green Subaru Forester. My suitcase kept straining to steer me around, like a dog pulling on a leash when it sees a squirrel. *Calm down, boy.* Bernie popped the car's back hatch and tossed my bag in.

"I've always wanted a Subaru," I said. Which wasn't just brown-nosing. When you're a broke grad student, you don't plan the names of your future children, but you do fantasize about the exact model and color of your first Subaru.

He opened the passenger door for me. "This is Jane's baby. She's got the Chevy this weekend. Not as much trunk room in there. My clothes fit in a duffle bag, but I wasn't sure how many suitcases you'd have with you."

There weren't any complimentary Fuji bottles waiting for me. There was a Vitaminwater in the cup holder, either half-empty or half-full depending on your disposition. A well-thumbed paperback with a cartoonish cover was lying on the passenger seat. *There Will Be Bud: A Cannabis Beach Bakeshop Mystery.*

"Is this Jane's, too?" I asked, picking it up. The only things I'd ever seen him read were congressional bills.

He shook his head. "You can throw that in the glove box. I just finished it waiting for your train. Not my favorite in the series, but you're welcome to read it. Cleared out one of those Little Free Libraries near our house. My neighbors had the whole series, except the newest one. Every time Jane and I walk past their house, I check to see if they've finished it." He sighed. "Slow readers."

I popped the glove box open. A pair of brown-and-white-striped mittens tumbled out into my lap. "Are these . . . ?"

"Mittens?" he said.

"*The* mittens?"

He started the engine. "You want to know if they're the mittens I wore to Biden's inauguration. That's all anyone wants to talk about these days: mittens, mittens, mittens. Nobody asks about the shoes I was wearing that day."

"What kind of shoes were they?"

"Brown," he said. "They were brown shoes."

The awkward silence that followed was my cue to stash everything back into the glove box and buckle my seat belt. I was acting like a nervous stan. Why had I asked about the mittens? I'd heard him lay into reporters asking about the inauguration memes, fed up with the media's focus on "gossip" when the world was on fire.

Once we were on the road, the tension in the car dissipated. Driving through the splendor that was Vermont in fall was as calming as a cup of chamomile tea spiked with melatonin. Bernie explained why he'd decided to drive me to Eagle Creek. He'd already been in Burlington, so it wasn't a big ask. Also, he was sick of lining the pockets of ride-sharing app executives. "Used to be, if you wanted to share a ride, you stood by the side of the road and stuck out your thumb," he said. "You know what that cost? Nothing! It was free. Silicon Valley took hitchhiking from the people and put a price tag on it. Uber's CEO received nearly $20 million in compensation last year. Where does the greed end?"

I kept my mouth shut, not wanting to embarrass myself further.

"You're from Eagle Creek," he said after a long silence. "Your mother runs the general store, right? I bet that was an experience, growing up."

Before I could answer, he turned up the radio. "Oh! It's past five. Do you mind?"

I told him to go for it, and for the next half hour we were serenaded by the dulcet tones of NPR's Ari Shapiro. I didn't mind. There would be plenty of time to stick my foot in my mouth this weekend. This was already the longest conversation I'd ever had with Bernie outside of my interview. The only time he'd said anything to me in the office was when he asked if I was going to finish the half-eaten whole-wheat bagel on my desk. When I said no, thinking he wanted the rest, he said, "You should. Lot of fiber in there."

The rush-hour traffic on the outskirts of Burlington—laughable by DC standards—gave way to long, empty stretches of highway in the country. The woods crowded the road from both sides, wild and untamed. The leaves were showing off with an arresting display of amber and vermillion and an array of hues I couldn't name without a color wheel. Vermont's beauty could be relentless this time of year. And since billboards were banned in the state, it didn't have to compete for your full attention.

Eagle Creek was three-quarters of the way up the eastern coast of Lake Champlain, the largest freshwater body in Vermont. We rolled into town at quarter to six. The highway went right through the center of town, doubling as the de facto Main Street. The posted speed limit was 23. Nobody knew why. And since this was Vermont, nobody was ever going to change it.

The welcome sign greeting visitors marked the city limits. Neither the mayor's name (Tamara Seeley) nor the town's population (2,853) had been updated since I'd last been here. In the case of the mayor, it didn't need to be. She'd been in office for more than forty years. The cost of repainting the sign weighed heavily on voters' minds.

My favorite part of the sign was the town's motto, in lovely internet brush script. "IF YOU LOVED HERE, YOU'D BE HOME ALREADY!" Not lived—*loved*. Ugh. It had been added within the last ten years but was already badly peeling. Nobody knew exactly what the phrase meant. And, because this was Vermont—say it with me—nobody was ever going to change it.

Eagle Creek was a cute little town, but I'd outgrown it. The white clapboard colonial houses lining the streets were as yawn-inducing as ever. The handful of businesses and city buildings downtown were the same as when I'd left for college: the art gallery, the DVD rental shop, the year-round Christmas store. A couple of dozen fishing boats were docked at the public marina. On the northern edge of town sat the library (open three days a week) and the county sheriff's department. Even at twenty-three miles per hour, you could drive through and miss the town . . . if it weren't for the Vermont Country Shed's twelve-by-eighteen-foot

American flag. Mom liked to say you could see it from space. At least the aliens would know where to land if they needed hard candy.

Bernie pulled right up to the store's entrance. There was a souped-up golf cart parked in the handicapped spot. It had thick tread on its tires, which were capped off with shiny chrome rims. The cart itself was Barbie pink. There wasn't a golf course within twenty miles, but the older folks liked to tool around in golf carts during the warmer months. And, of course, it gave bored kids something to do during the summer. Stealing golf carts was a rite of passage in Eagle Creek.

"Stopping for groceries first?" I asked Bernie. I hadn't planned on seeing my mother just yet, but if he wanted something to eat that hadn't been sitting all day under a gas station heat lamp, the general store was the only option. Unless you counted the Moose Knuckle brew pub. All they served were tater tots, which could sop up booze but did little to stave off hunger.

Bernie pulled his phone out of his shirt pocket. "The map says this is the bed-and-breakfast. The Eagle's Nest B&B. But this is your mother's general store, isn't it?"

I checked the itinerary I'd downloaded earlier. I'd also printed a copy out in case I dropped my phone in the lake. Or threw it into the lake, if I got one more spam text telling me I'D WON! TODAY'S! IPAD! CONTEST! Nice try, Putin. This girl wasn't going to be the weak link who got phished inside the Sanders office.

The store's address was indeed listed under the name of the B&B. I'd never heard of an "Eagle's Nest" anything around here. A quick internet search yielded no hits in the surrounding area.

Heck, there wasn't an Eagle's Nest in the state according to the Google machine.

"If anyone knows where the B&B is, it will be my mother," I said, unbuckling my seat belt. "I'll get the address and be right back faster than you can say 'Jeezum Crow.'"

Jeezum Crow? I hadn't been in the Green Mountain State an hour yet, and already I'd gone full Vermont. It was only a matter of time before I started wearing flannel again. Not that I'd be opposed. The sun had set, and there was now a slight chill in the air. From somewhere distant, the smell of burning leaves drifted on the breeze. Flannel shirts were made for nights like this.

It wasn't until I was on the porch that I realized I'd already broken the first rule of Bernie Club. Oh well. Lana couldn't have expected me to keep my eyes on Bernie literally every minute of the weekend. Sure, she'd said "literally," but everyone misuses that word to mean "figuratively." I'd only be inside for a few minutes. If Bernie wanted to stretch his legs, how far could he go?

Chapter 4

The screen door swung shut behind me with a bang. In the morning, the booths would have been filled with regulars sipping coffee and reading the *Burlington Free Press*. Not at this hour. Six o'clock was closing time in small-town Vermont. In the summer it was strange to see the town close down with hours of sunlight left, but in the fall it sort of made sense.

The only customers left in the dining area tonight were the Blooming sisters, Edwina and Maude. The identical twins were co-owners of Everything's Maple, the maple gift shop a few paces down the road. The white-haired sisters looked up from their knitting only briefly, but it was still long enough to cast silent judgment with a couple of smirks. They remembered what a handful I'd been for my mother in high school, always demanding to be driven down to Burlington for some protest march or another.

"We're about to close, so make it quick," my mother shouted from the front counter without looking up. Her face was buried in that book about singing crawdads. Hadn't read it myself. The only books I'd read over the past couple of years were assigned texts.

I approached the counter. "What's a crawdad sound like?"

My mother jerked her head up. It looked like I'd startled her out of her Birkenstocks. She stared at me blankly, but her shock quickly turned to delight. "Crash!" she shrieked, rounding the counter to embrace me. As we hugged, I felt the lower back brace she'd begun wearing a few years ago.

"I didn't know if you were coming," she said. "All I have in the fridge is Yankee pot roast, but I know how you feel about roast beef."

"The same way I feel about all meat."

"I know, I know. 'It's murder.'"

"Could be worse," I said. "I could be vegan."

She lifted my chin. "Let me have a look at you . . . Oh, look at that. You're still my baby girl. Even if you're all dressed up."

Was I? It was my go-to business casual look, a pleated skirt and Peter Pan collar blouse. "I would have called, but I've been so busy," I said. "Work, school. You know."

A bearded man with an eyepatch set a Styrofoam container on the counter. It was Doc McGilliam. His long hair was pulled into a single braid that ran down his back. He was wearing a Vermont tuxedo—a fleece vest over a flannel shirt.

"Just the crawlers," Doc said to my mother, holding up the container so she could see. "Though it's highway robbery, if you ask me."

She laughed. "Ain't no robbery, and you know it. Two bucks for a dozen worms is as good as you'll find on the lake. I'll add it to your tab. Go on."

He laughed like the pack-a-day smoker he'd been for thirty years before quitting. I could smell the Nicorette on his breath.

As he turned to leave, he almost slammed right into me. "Dang, Crash, either you're getting taller or I'm getting shorter."

"A little of column A, a little of column B," I said, pretty sure it was mostly column B. I'd stalled out at five-four my sophomore year of high school.

Doc patted me on the shoulder. "Heard you were in DC fighting for us little guys," he said. "We're real proud of you, Crash."

I smiled and thanked him, although most days I didn't feel like I was fighting for anyone or anything but my sanity. Doc started to leave but my mother stopped him with a holler. "Oh, I almost forgot. Ferman Fletcher was in here yesterday asking about you. Said you needed to stop by the bank and talk to him. I told him I wasn't about to be a go-between—Ferman can do his own dirty work—but he said it was urgent."

Doc snorted. "I've got two words and a knuckle sandwich for him, but I'm not going to serve either of them in public."

Doc was an easygoing guy, generally. It took a lot to tick off a Vermont hippie. The manager of the Eagle Creek Savings & Loan had apparently done it, though. Overdraft fees, I assumed. They could get to the best of us.

When he was gone, my mother apologized to me. "So, where's the man of the hour?" She covered her mouth, realizing she'd slipped up. "Sorry, I forgot nobody's supposed to know he's in town. My lips are sealed until tomorrow."

Edwina and Maude were still knitting at their table, pretending not to eavesdrop. You had to watch what you said around them. Hollywood had TMZ; Eagle Creek had the Blooming sisters.

"He's waiting on me in the parking lot," I told my mother. "I can't talk long. I'm actually stopping in for directions, right now. We're trying to find an Eagle's Nest bed-and-breakfast?"

She gently cackled. "That's just some silly name I made up for tax purposes. You like it? It's not much of a B&B. If I'd known you were going to be staying here tonight, I would have put up some of your old posters. They're all in the basement."

I glared at her. "You turned my room into a bed-and-breakfast."

"And the guest bedroom. But like I said, it's not much. Breakfast is in the dining room here downstairs, so it's not as fancy as it sounds. You weren't visiting enough to use your room, and the guest room was only being used for storage ever since your cousin moved out to his own place. So why not?"

"Why not, Mom? Let me tell you why . . . not . . ." I felt a familiar brush against my leg, and then another. It was Selena Gomez (our black cat, not the singer-slash-actor). I scooped her up, giving her a bear hug. She didn't resist, not like when she'd been a kitten. We were both old souls now. "I need to get back to the senator. He's probably wondering if I've gotten lost."

My mother handed me the keys to the rooms we'd be staying in upstairs. Never had a key for my room when I'd lived here, but I could have used one. What kid wouldn't want the ability to lock their own door to prevent snooping parents?

As I stepped back outside, a flash of silver above the tree line caught my eye. There it was again—zipping back and forth over the wooded hills behind the general store. A second flash joined it. Aliens? No. Just a pair of hobbyist drones flying low, circling each other before disappearing below the canopy. A little high-tech for a town still waiting on high-speed internet. Someone was bound to shoot them out of the sky soon enough.

Bernie had parked at the far edge of the parking lot, near the tent that had been set up in advance of tomorrow's kickoff festivities. I read the banner. "CHAMP DAYS . . . Presented by Maplewood Springs® Traditional Vermont Syrup." What would

Bernie say about the festival being sponsored by some faceless corporate agribusiness? It turned out I would have to wait for the answer. The Subaru was empty.

Bernie was missing.

Okay, Crash. Deep breath.

I'd been gone longer than I'd intended, but not that long. As we say in Vermont, it hadn't been longer than a donkey's ears. Where could he have gone? The lights were out at the co-op art gallery. Farther down the road, the DVD rental store's neon OPEN sign was turned off. Eagle Creek wasn't big enough to get lost in. Believe me, I'd tried as a teenager. The woods were another story, but I didn't think Bernie would have entered them on his own. That was an easy way for your face to end up on a milk carton.

I dialed his cell. No answer.

Should I call Lana? No, she'd already made it known she wouldn't pick up under any circumstances. She would be too sloshed to answer. If things went really sideways, however, she'd given me a ripcord to pull. I found the business card in my wallet, the one on which she'd scribbled a number with a Vermont area code.

Do you know what a fixer is? she'd said, handing it to me at the office.

I said I'd seen *Scandal.* That and *Veep* were required viewing for prospective poli-sci students.

Only call this number in case of an emergency. But I have to let you know, there's a price for calling it. And that price is your internship. So, life and death situations only.

I returned the card to my wallet. I wasn't ready to use it, not yet. Hopefully, not ever.

After looking both ways, I jogged across the highway to the marina. If Bernie had gone for a walk, he would have headed straight for the water. Old people love lakes.

I walked the rickety planks of one of the wooden docks to the end. I wanted to get a good look both ways down the rocky shore. The dock swayed under my feet. I turned around and scanned the coast. No sign of the boss. No sign of anybody. The only sign of life was a large yacht anchored just north of downtown. It was the biggest boat I'd ever seen on Lake Champlain. Were the One Percent settling down in Eagle Creek, or just visiting?

The best course of action was to return to the parking lot and wait. Eventually, he'd find his way back—

I froze. A dark shape was floating on the surface between two docked steel fishing boats, bobbing up and down, up and down. Not a shape—a person. Facedown, with a yellow hood covering the back of their head. Panic inched up my spine. Bernie hadn't been wearing a jacket, but who was to say he hadn't thrown one on to go for a walk?

I borrowed an oar from the nearest boat and reached it into the water, snagging the weed-covered jacket. I dragged the body closer, closer, until it was finally within reach. With a steadying breath, I flipped it over and gasped as I recognized the drowned man's shocked face.

Why didn't I listen to my suitcase when I had the chance?

I should have never come back to Eagle Creek.

Chapter 5

When the sheriff's deputy arrived, I was still standing on the waterfront trying to process what had happened. She rushed past me straight to the end of the dock, where a trio of volunteer fire-fighters had already pulled the body out of the water. They were standing around it, as if they'd just landed the catch of a lifetime. It was, in a way. The body was Mr. Fletcher's. The town banker my mother was passing messages for.

The firefighters had been first on the scene. They'd already been outside the firehouse, waxing their truck for Monday's parade. I didn't know whether an ambulance or helicopter had been dispatched from Burlington. It didn't matter much. Paramedics wouldn't be able to do anything. Mr. Fletcher's face had been drained of all color by the time I'd found him. It didn't take a medical examiner to know he was dead, and had been for some time.

After squatting to examine the body, the deputy returned my way. Another familiar face, but this time it was a welcome one. Rhea Kelly. The sheriff's daughter. She'd been a grade below me.

I'd always liked her, even if we'd never been besties. (That may have had something to do with my views on the need for policing reform.) Rhea's fair-skinned cheeks were still dotted with freckles, and her strawberry-blond hair was, as always, braided into two long pigtails.

"Crash," she said, looking just as surprised as I was. "When did you get into town?"

"Less than a half hour ago," I said. "It's nice to be back in Vermont. I mean, except for the dead guy."

"That's some bad luck right there. What did you do, cross a black cat on your way into town?"

"Just Selena Gomez," I said. "But she's always been good luck. This has been the weirdest day of my life by far."

She laughed. "You sound all funny," she said. "You went and got yourself an accent."

What she meant was I didn't have a Vermont accent anymore. It was one of the first things I'd lost at college. "A couple of beers, and I start dropping my T's," I said. "Anyway, I'm just in town for Champ Days."

"Finally reentering the Maple Queen contest?" she teased.

The town was still doing that? It wasn't as sexist as other pageants—instead of a swimsuit round, potential Maple Queens faced off in a flannel competition. My mother, a three-time Maple Queen finalist in her middle school days, entered me when I was ten. I gave a speech rejecting the male gaze. *I am a woman, not an object,* I'd said. For the talent portion, I karate-chopped a pine board in half. To hear my mother tell the story, you'd think half the judges wet themselves when that wood snapped.

Only one did.

Unfortunately, it was the mayor.

I didn't win.

I didn't have to remind Rhea of any of this, because she'd won handily that year. Her speech was an impassioned defense of the Second Amendment.

Presently, a crowd had begun to form on the dock. And by "crowd," I mean twenty or so people. Sheer pandemonium by Eagle Creek standards. Rhea told me to head back to the general store, that someone would be by later to take a statement. I'd left out any mention about the AWOL Bernie Sanders. I couldn't risk Bernie's name ending up on a police report somewhere. That was a fast way to lose not just my internship, but any political future I hoped to have.

I kept my head down as I filed past the onlookers, trying not to make eye contact with anyone else. The Blooming sisters were sitting in their pink golf cart on the highway shoulder. This had to be like Christmas morning for them. *First, Terri Robertson's girl comes home for a visit—unexpectedly, from the sound of things— and the next thing you know she's fishing for cadavers.*

Once they learned Bernie was in town, their white-haired heads would catch fire.

Where had Bernie gone? The Subaru was right where he'd left it, empty, abandoned. What was he thinking, heading off without me or the security detail that would be joining us in the morning? Sure, he hadn't been mobbed at the train station, but that was because passengers were wrapped up in their own little worlds. I had a feeling that his dad cap wasn't going to disguise him in Eagle Creek, where outsiders were heavily scrutinized. The fixer's card was burning a hole in my handbag. I would check first with my mother. If she hadn't seen Bernie, it was a distinct possibility that my weekend—and my internship—would be coming to an abrupt end.

The shades were drawn back at the store, but I could hear voices inside. The door was locked. I didn't want to go all the way around to the back stairs and through the guest quarters, so I knocked on the door and stepped back.

My cousin Tyler answered. His skin was tanned, his hair short and spiky. He was in red flannel. Typical. Tyler had only two looks: lumberjack, and—when the thermometer flirted with ninety—shirtless lumberjack.

"Cuz!" he said, pulling me in for a hug. He might have graduated from high school two years ago, but he hadn't graduated from the Axe Body Spray. There was another smell, though, one I hadn't smelled in years.

"Is that . . . maple syrup?" I asked, sniffing at his gelled hair. I'd known guys in undergrad who shampooed with beer, but this was ridiculous. I went to run my fingers through his hair, and he pulled back sharply.

"Maple hair gel," he said. "Wicked hold, but it's a little sticky."

"You don't say."

"C'mon in," he said. "We've been waiting for you."

As soon as I stepped into the store, the warmth from the fireplace welcomed me with open arms. I realized why Bernie wasn't in his car. He was seated at one of the dining tables. I almost fainted from relief. As I approached him, I smelled something baking back in the kitchen. It had been too long since I'd had anything not from a microwave.

"Were you trying to call me?" Bernie asked. "I don't have your number, and you didn't leave a message. I figured maybe you were one of those robo-callers. Robots are even putting telemarketers out of work."

I told him it was my number, so he could program it into his phone. I took a seat at the table. I'd been on my feet for an hour. It shouldn't have felt that good to take a load off, but it did.

"What's that smell?" I asked him, assuming he'd ordered supper.

"Your mother's cooking harvest stuffed squash and apple griddlecakes. I asked for the house special, and she said she'd do me one better with a couple of off-menu items."

Although I was glad to have discovered I hadn't lost my boss, it was worrying how quickly he'd been adopted by my family in my absence. Mom's special griddlecakes? She only cooked those for me on my birthday.

"Did you all notice the emergency vehicles outside?" I said. There'd been no sirens, but it should have been hard to ignore all the flashing lights across the highway.

Tyler and Bernie looked at each other, then shook their heads. Bernie had a voice trained to drown out screaming crowds, and my cousin had the hearing of someone who'd been working with power tools since he was seven. Between the two of them—and my mother, yelling from the kitchen—you wouldn't have been able to hear an F5 sharknado tearing up the town.

My mother came out of the kitchen and announced that dinner would be ready in twenty-five minutes. While I worried what childhood stories she might try to tell Bernie, at least she wouldn't embarrass me with her culinary skills.

I took a seat across from Bernie.

My boss was seated at my family dining table.

Was that more or less surreal than finding a body?

In fact, the entire day had taken a surreal turn the moment we'd slowed to twenty-three miles an hour. It was wild how little the store had changed. It still had that same, strange mishmash of products, from kitchen utensils to jars of cinnamon sticks, from dreamcatchers to double-A batteries. None of it was random, however. The inventory was uniquely tailored to the local clientele and, in every season but mud season, tourists passing through. I'd once imagined the store was the last of its kind, like Champ.

And it had been once upon a time, back when my great-grand-parents had opened it in nineteen-whatever. Nowadays, there was a throwback general store in every New England town. They might have been knockoffs, but they were better than the Dollar Generals down in Virginia.

I told my cousin and the senator about finding the banker's body. I left out the part that I'd been strolling the dock searching for Bernie—who, apparently, had done a lap around the general store and then entered, looking for me. My mother had offered him a chair, and they'd been waiting for me to return ever since. The one who'd been "lost" the whole time was me.

"I would have just called the body in, anonymous-like," Tyler said. "Who wants to wait around with some dead guy for the cops to show up?"

"The police have caller ID," I said. "Hard to be anonymous these days."

"I'd block it. And use an app to disguise my voice."

In my best creepy voice, I said, "What's your favorite scary movie?" The blank look on his face told me my mother still hadn't subjected him to the *Scream* movies.

There was a knock at the door. Tyler started to get up, but I told him I'd get it. They were supposed to be sending a detective by to talk to me. When I opened the door, I was standing face-to-face with Joey Blackheart. As in, my ex-boyfriend from the ninth grade Joey Blackheart. And, based on the badge clipped to his belt, Detective Joey Blackheart.

"Heck of a homecoming, Crash," he said without a hint of irony. He had the same cop mustache he'd had since eighth grade. "What are you doing back here?"

"Work trip with my boss."

His mouth fell open and he pushed past me. "Wait, is that Bernie Sanders?"

Bernie held up a forkful of griddlecake in greeting.

"Yeah," I said, crossing my arms. "That's my boss."

Chapter 6

I didn't think my family—or Bernie—wanted to hear any more about what I'd seen, so I led Joey around the store to the back stoop. He whipped out a small black Moleskine. Not exactly your standard-issue law enforcement notebook. I was glad to see that, despite the badge, he was still the same sensitive kid I'd known all those years ago.

"I can't believe you're a cop," I blurted out. "Sorry. Didn't mean it like that."

He laughed. "I'm with the state's Major Crimes Unit. We only deal with the fun cases. You know, murders. Kidnappings. I never have to pull anyone over for a busted headlight."

"Are there really that many murders in this state?"

"Around a dozen a year," he said. "You ever hear of the Green Mountain Madman?"

"I listened to a podcast about him. Just horrible what he did to those campers. Were you the one who caught him?"

"I wish," Joey said with a wistful sigh. "All I'm saying is, it does happen in Vermont. Not often, thank God. Most of the calls we take are for suspicious deaths, which usually turn out to be overdoses. Normally, we'll wait for the medical examiner's report before doing any legwork. Just so happens I was in town already, visiting my parents. Champ Days is this weekend, you know."

"That's sort of why I'm here."

"Sort of?"

"Well, it's why Bernie's here and why I'm with him. We're trying to keep his presence under wraps until his first event tomorrow morning, so if you could keep it on the DL, that would be super helpful."

"Can do," he promised. Having once gotten to second base with a state detective had its perks. "Remember when we volunteered for him? You ever see that volunteer coordinator again?"

"The one you described as being 'hotter than Harry Styles in a locker room sauna'?" I shook my head. "He was from out of state. New Hampshire, if I remember. I'll let you know if I see him around, though. There's no conflict between your job and you being, y'know . . ."

". . . into Harry Styles?"

"You know what I mean. I can't imagine."

"If it makes you feel any better, I march every year in Burlington Pride in full uniform," he said. "Nobody on the force has said a thing about me being gay. Being a ginger, on the other hand . . ."

That was refreshing to hear—both the part about his colleagues and that he had a firm grasp on who he was. His teenage years had been a difficult and confusing time. I'd blamed myself for a few weeks after we broke up, thinking I'd done something to turn him off girls. *Don't flatter yourself,* he'd messaged me once we were on speaking terms again. *You're a bad kisser, but not THAT bad.*

I'd worked a lot on my kissing game since then. Who knew you weren't supposed to try to lick your partner's wisdom teeth clean?

Joey capped his pen. "Anything else? I've got a few other interviews to conduct tonight, but I'd love to catch up once this is all sorted."

There was one other thing I'd been holding on to. I'd been afraid to mention that Mr. Fletcher had been looking for Doc, because it wasn't my business. Doc was just an old hippie. He was everything Eagle Creek stood for: peace, nature, and Vermont maple syrup. But the truth would come out sooner or later. Especially since the Blooming sisters had been in the store, too.

"It's probably nothing," I said, "but Mr. Fletcher was looking for Doc. Said it was urgent." Doc had tensed up at the mention of Mr. Fletcher's name. Not his usual, mellow self. He'd quit smoking years ago, but still smoked (if you catch my drift). The Doc I'd seen in the store earlier could have used a toke.

Joey shrugged. "I'll make a note of that here, just in case," he said. "You're probably right about it being nothing, though. Mr. Fletcher's fishing boat is missing and he wasn't wearing a life jacket. And you know how cold the lake is this time of year. Even if he was a decent swimmer, his arms and legs would eventually go numb due to the cold shock. Then he'd start to sink, and . . ." He made a croaking noise. "The medical examiner's office is down in Burlington. We'll know more once she completes her report."

"How long does that usually take?" I asked.

"An initial report? Twenty-four hours. If she needs to do an autopsy or toxicology? Then we're talking weeks." Joey snapped his notebook closed. "I've seen it take months."

As we'd been speaking, guilt had been creeping up in the back of my mind, and it had nothing to do with narcing on Doc. Why hadn't I at least tried to maintain a friendship with Joey through college? It hadn't been intentional. I'd just . . . made no effort. I was all about making new friends. Making a new life.

He'd come to Washington once, "just driving through." The summer after my freshman year. I hadn't returned his texts. The only news I'd heard about Joey since then was that he was working down in Burlington now. That's all my mother had said. She'd never told me what he was doing there. Not that I'd asked. If she'd said he was entering the police academy, would I have tried to come home and talk him out of it? Ultimately, Joey was as selfless a person as I'd ever known. The world needed more good cops.

"How long are you in town for?" he said, slapping at a mosquito on his neck.

"I leave Monday night," I said. "Honestly, this was sort of a last-minute trip. I want to catch up, but don't know if I'll have the time. Senator Sanders has events scheduled one after the other, beginning tomorrow morning. I'm not supposed to leave him alone. Maybe next time."

"Yeah," he said. "Maybe next time."

He returned to his car. We'd talked for close to an hour. He hadn't even tried to hide his disappointment in me. Couldn't he see that I literally wouldn't have the time this weekend? And didn't he have any "fun" murders to solve?

When I went back inside, a to-go box with my supper was waiting for me at the table. My mother told me that Bernie had gone upstairs for the night and my cousin was in the kitchen cleaning up. Tyler worked part-time in the general store, so he knew his way around back there. That was when he wasn't doing contracting work around town, of course. If you needed painting, woodwork, or construction in Eagle Creek, Tyler was your guy.

"You didn't tell any embarrassing stories about me, did you?" I asked my mother. "Get out a photo album and show him my baby pictures?"

"All your baby photos are on my phone now. Your cousin scanned them for me. I can send you a link—it's in a cloud somewhere," she said. "Bernie's quite the talker. He had a lot to say about you."

That was surprising, since I didn't think he'd been keeping tabs on me or any of the interns. I couldn't let my mother know this, though. Didn't want to ruin the image she'd built in her head of me and the senator, sipping hot cocoa and working on a minimum wage bill late into the night.

"I hope he said good things," I told her.

"He mentioned you barely said a word on the car ride here. I said, 'That sounds like my Crash. Always with her head someplace else.'"

"Mom. You didn't say that."

"It's true, no?" She stood. "You can eat down here if you want—just turn out the lights when you're done. I'd imagine you're tired, but I don't know if I could sleep if I'd seen someone drowned in the lake."

"Do you think they'll cancel Champ Days?"

My mother laughed. "If it were a tourist, maybe. It wouldn't be great publicity. But this is Ferman. Not the most popular man in town. No one's going to let him ruin their weekend." She gave me another hug, this time even longer than the last. "I'm just glad you're home. See you bright and early."

Bernie had brought my bag in and set it next to the door for me. I took my food upstairs. The key didn't fit the door to my room, however. The number on the key chain and the door didn't match up. Crud. When I'd left the keys on the table, Bernie must have grabbed the key to my old room. He was a notorious night owl, keeping staff up late into the night while on the road. I could hear him on the phone with his wife through the door. Hopefully, my mother had redecorated my room since I'd left, because I did not want to answer questions about where one would even begin to find Ed Sheeran drapes.

The internet. The answer is always the internet.

The guest room I'd drawn was done up like a cabin, complete with flannel sheets and a painting of a family of loons lounging on the water. The picture window looked out over the marina. I immediately closed the curtains. I brushed my teeth in the small attached bathroom, staring too long at myself in the mirror. My shoulder-length hair was a bird's nest. It looked like I'd spent half the day in an oversold train. Now I understood why Bernie was always going on about high-speed bullet trains. Better for the country. Better for my hair.

I turned on the lamp beside the king-size bed and got under the thick comforter. The windows were open, and a cool breeze passed through the room. Emails had been piling up in my inbox for the past few hours. I read the important ones, and then got distracted by YouTube. Okay, I went down a full YouTube hole and was soon giggling at cat videos. My mother's Wi-Fi was screaming fast, compared to when I'd left for school. Just like Eagle Creek to wait until I was gone to wade into the twenty-first century and get real broadband.

Before I turned out the light, I decided to check out the mystery novel Bernie had lent to me. His review of the book hadn't been super enthusiastic, but I had time to kill while waiting for my gummies to knock me out. I flipped to the back cover to get an idea of what I was getting myself into. Cozies weren't my usual genre.

Cannabis bakeshop owner Mary-Jane Taylor returns in There Will Be Bud, *the latest Cannon Cove mystery from the bestselling author of* Murder by the Gram.

Everything's coming up green for the Cannabis Beach Bakeshop, the artisanal edibles bakery that Mary-Jane Taylor inherited from her late grandmother. Thanks to a flattering front-page review in the Oregon Coast Times, *customers have been making the pilgrimage from all over the Pacific Northwest for Mary-Jane's culinary creations.*

Not everyone is happy with the growing traffic, however. Tensions are rising in the picture-perfect small town, leading to a contentious chamber of commerce meeting where battle lines are drawn in the sand between friends and neighbors.

When Douglas Knox, the proprietor of the year-round Christmas store and ringleader of the growing anti-tourist sentiment in town, is found murdered, Mary-Jane's handsome baking assistant, Bud Majors, is fingered as the culprit. She puts her mortgage on the line to post his bail. If she can't clear Bud's name, will the high-flying days of the Cannabis Beach Bakeshop be at an end?

People read this stuff? I thought, though by the second page I was hooked. I made it halfway through the first chapter when it became impossible to keep my eyes open any longer. The mysteries of Cannon Cove would have to wait for another day. Which was fine by me—I'd had enough of dead bodies in small towns for one day. As I drifted off, it wasn't Mr. Fletcher's face that surfaced in my mind's eye. It was Doc's. He was looking at me questioningly, wondering why I'd given him up to the cops.

Chapter 7

The itinerary called for Bernie's stint "working" at the general store on Saturday morning to last from ten until noon. I planned to sleep in until eight thirty or so, which would give me some time to prepare before Bernie rolled out of bed and wandered downstairs. He was a late riser. If he was in the office before ten in the morning, it meant something was amiss in the world. Other than the usual economic, racial, social, and environmental issues, of course.

My plans were shattered by my mother clanging around in the kitchen, which was directly below the guest room. I glanced at my phone. A few minutes before eight. How had my cousin ever slept in here? I rolled over and buried my face in the pillow, but it was no use. Between my mother prepping food in the kitchen and the lingering image of Mr. Fletcher on the lake, I wasn't getting any more shuteye this morning.

I threw on a T-shirt and jeans and went downstairs. To my shock, Bernie was already behind the register with a Vermont

Country Shed apron on. Something was amiss in the world, alright. He was fiddling with the antique cash register. A woman I didn't recognize was waiting for him to make change.

"This thing is older than my brother Larry," Bernie complained, pushing the cash drawer closed again. It popped right back open. "Just as much of a fussbudget, too."

The customer smiled brightly at this. She had on a worn denim shirt and a pair of mud boots. It smelled like she'd been walking through more than mud this morning.

"Larry Sanders is your brother?" she asked Bernie.

He looked up. "What, he owe you money or something?"

She shook her head. "Oh, no. My hubby and I just love that show of his on HBO."

Bernie quit messing with the register. He pulled a couple of coins out of his own pocket. "Different Larry Sanders," he mumbled, slapping her change down. Her face grew as red as her shirt, and she scuttled off. Bernie usually reserved his ire for those who deserved it: greedy corporations, corrupt businessmen, and former Federal Reserve chairman Alan Greenspan. Now I could add "antique cash registers" and "fans of Garry Shandling's fictional talk-show host Larry Sanders" to that list.

Bernie was pricklier than most politicians, but he enjoyed meeting the public. During Senate recesses, Bernie liked to get out there on the road and talk to his constituents one-on-one. Scoop some ice cream, milk some cows. It was a chance to discuss his legislative priorities directly with voters. He couldn't do it on his own, however. Especially with a finicky register. Thankfully, it was unusually dead for this hour.

"I'm going upstairs to change, and I'll be right back down," I told Bernie.

"Something wrong with what you have on?"

"This is a work function," I said. "The dress code—"

"Change if you want, but this isn't Washington. I'd be in jeans, too, but they're in the wash. Had a little accident with a bottle of mustard last night."

He had on a rumpled navy suit. The best thing I could say about it was that it wasn't his rumpled gray suit.

I slipped into the kitchen. My mother was working the grill. "Don't you have anyone else scheduled today?" I said, raising my voice over the sound of the bacon fat popping. "Senator Sanders is going to be mobbed up front when people find out he's here. There'll be a line for the checkout all the way back to the ice cream freezer."

"He has you," my mother said.

"He wasn't supposed to start until ten."

She cracked an egg on the griddle. "He was waiting in the dining area reading when I came downstairs to start the coffee. He seems to be doing okay out there. I asked if we should wake you, and he said to let you sleep. On account of what happened last night."

I couldn't fault them for worrying about me. It *was* the first dead body I'd ever found.

"Who's supposed to be on the schedule today to help you?" I asked. "It's Champ Days. The tourists, the traffic . . ."

"The labor market around here isn't what it used to be. The townspeople are getting older. Every year there are fewer and fewer high schoolers. I make do around here best as I can. Your cousin lends a hand, but most days it's just me."

When I was growing up, she'd had a rotating staff of local teenagers. In the summers, students could pick up even more hours. I'd been one of those kids, albeit the one who got paid the least. Funny thing: minimum wage laws don't apply to family businesses.

Bernie poked his head through the kitchen doors like that poster of Jack Nicholson in *The Shining*—*Here's Bernie!* "Looks like we're out of light-roast coffee."

I told him I would start a fresh brew. If things were going to go smoothly this morning, I was going to have to help out around the store. I would have to bag groceries, and stock shelves, and take orders. The life of a personal aide on the road was shaping up to be less glamorous than I'd imagined. *Acting* personal aide, I reminded myself. I was still an intern. Nobody ever said an intern's life was supposed to be easy.

Before I could start the coffee, the bells over the door jangled. Joey was back. He was in full uniform this time, complete with a wide-brimmed state trooper hat. Was he here for me? I'd told him everything I knew, exactly as it had happened. I also knew detectives often re-interviewed witnesses because memory was a funny thing. *They also re-interviewed suspects.*

"Sorry I'm late," he said, meeting me at the register. "I was asleep when I got the call."

"The call?"

"Rhea—who was supposed to be here, temping off-duty for you guys—is still working the drowning investigation. It's her first suspicious death, so her dad wants her to see it through. I told the sheriff I'd take her shift with the senator."

Letting "the new girl" follow a case to closure because it was "her first"? That didn't sound like how law enforcement agencies were supposed to work. It definitely wasn't how the Sanders office operated. But this was Eagle Creek.

"Has she gotten anywhere, yet?" I asked.

"Turns out Mr. Fletcher never showed up to work yesterday morning. Didn't call in or answer his phone. Co-workers said he'd been acting strange lately. Stressed. Like somebody trying to hide an addiction. He allegedly had an online gambling problem, too. I asked your mother if he bought any alcohol when he came in here Thursday, but she said all he bought was corn syrup. Anyway, several witnesses saw him drinking at the brew pub late Thursday night. Close to ten o'clock. That might clinch it, right there."

"That's awful," I said, although what I really felt was relief. If it was an accident, whatever bad blood had been between Doc and Mr. Fletcher was beside the point. My conscience was off the hook. Whether I'd be able to look Doc in the eye again, knowing I'd given his name up to Joey . . . that was another story.

Customer traffic picked up a little over the next couple of hours. Not by much, though. I had time to show Bernie how to close the register without it popping back open. And I was on high alert for any more mentions of either Larry Sanders. I also gave Bernie a crash course in the fine art of grocery bagging. For somebody who'd never worked retail a day in his life, Bernie showed no signs of tiring on his feet. After all, the man knew a thing or two about comfortable footwear, having once delivered an eight-and-a-half-hour filibuster speech in the Senate—without a bathroom break.

I glanced at the clock on the wall. Quarter after eleven. Time wasn't just moving slow this morning, it was moving in reverse. If things continued at this pace, there wasn't enough caffeine in the state to keep my eyes open all the way until the end of Bernie's "shift," which was a long forty-five minutes away.

"It's a meet-and-greet, no advance publicity," Bernie said, noticing me staring at the clock. "Things will pick up. I remember when I formally announced my candidacy for president, first time around. In Burlington, we had five thousand supporters. A couple of weeks later in Madison, Wisconsin, we had ten thousand. And the number kept growing, from city to city. Point is, it usually takes a little while for word of mouth to spread."

"Might be tough, with the Beefcake Breakfast," Joey said.

We both turned to him at the end of the counter, where he'd been standing silently all morning. I'd practically forgotten he was there. "The firefighters' pancake breakfast isn't until tomorrow," I reminded him. "Today's Saturday."

"The Champ Days committee had to move some things around to accommodate the senator's events," Joey explained. "I guarantee you that's where everyone is, tourists included. The line at the firehouse was already wrapped around the block when I passed it this morning."

"We're being outdrawn by flapjacks," Bernie said. I thought I detected an audible note of defeat in his voice, but just barely.

"Flapjacks and shirtless firefighters," I said, trying to give Bernie's ego a small boost.

"And Jagger Wardlow," Joey said.

The Jagger Wardlow? What was the billionaire tech guru doing at Eagle Creek's pancake breakfast? The last I'd heard of him, he'd sold off his app to Google, who stripped its source code and killed it. He should have been living it up in the tropics, not bumming around rural Vermont.

"Jagger?" Joey said. "The Maplewood Springs guy? You've probably seen his boat on the lake. It's the only one big enough to land a helicopter on."

Bernie shoved the cash drawer in. This time it stuck. "Is this firehouse in walking distance?" he asked.

I nodded. "I can run over and grab you some pancakes to go."

"We're almost finished here," he said. "Then we can swing by. Wouldn't want to miss the 'beefcakes.'"

Or Jagger Wardlow, I thought. Bernie Sanders and a billionaire in the same room. It had disaster written all over it. Forget jumping out of the frying pan and into the fire. I'd just been thrown from the fire into an erupting volcano.

Chapter 8

By the time we arrived at the firehouse, the line outside had dissipated. Several dozen people were still seated inside, chowing down. It was a sea of dad caps and Karen cuts. All profits went to the volunteer fire department, which made the twenty-five-dollar tickets easier to stomach. The all-you-can-eat bonanza featured scrambled eggs, bacon, and sausage. Make no mistake, though, the pancakes were the main attraction. They weren't my mother's apple griddlecakes, but they were up there.

At the door, Bernie took his wallet out to pay for tickets for me and Joey. Lana had said the office would reimburse me for meals, but Bernie wasn't having that. "My treat," he said.

As Bernie was finding exact change, a bearded man in dark sunglasses emerged from the building. He was wearing a pair of firefighter's overalls, with both straps down. Underneath, he was shirtless. He had the sort of baby-oil-slathered abs that only billionaires could buy.

"Senator Sanders," Wardlow said, holding out a sweaty hand to shake. "I hadn't realized you were going to be in town, Senator. I'd love to show you around the Maplewood Springs facilities this weekend, if you have time."

Bernie looked at the hand but didn't shake it.

"We don't," he said gruffly, snatching the tickets.

The firefighters were working the griddles in helmets, aprons, swim trunks . . . and nothing else. I'd never been able to bring myself to call it the "Beefcake Breakfast." First: gross. I didn't need to see my classmates' dads half-naked. Second: not to bodyshame, but their dad bods did not exactly scream "beefcake."

We sat down at one of the long tables inside with our plates stacked high. There were a few double takes, but no one approached us. Bernie picked up the plastic syrup bottle in the middle of the table. He turned it around so we could see the logo. Maplewood Springs. The logo was everywhere in the firehouse—on banners, on napkins, and probably even on the toilet paper in the outhouses out front. People were helping themselves to free Maplewood-branded tie-dyed hoodies from a table set up in the back. Free T-shirts were one thing, but free hoodies? I couldn't help but question Jagger's "generosity."

"Native Americans were the first to tap trees in this nation," Bernie said, staring at the plastic bottle as if it were a rattler about to bite him. "The techniques haven't changed much. Now Mr. Wardlow swoops in and starts buying up struggling maple farms. He's already amassed more taps under one company than any other sugarmaker this side of the Canadian border. It's not on the front page of the *New York Times*, but that doesn't mean it's not a crisis. This could be the dawn of Big Maple in Vermont."

Prior to Maplewood Springs, few multinational corporations had judged the maple syrup industry worthy of takeover. The margins were too slim, the work too hard. Leave it to a Silicon Valley bro to flip the tables. He must have found some technological advantage over the family-owned maple farms.

"You knew he was sponsoring Champ Days when you accepted the invitation," I said. "You were expecting some sort of confrontation."

"I had a good idea he'd be in town this weekend. I wanted to come over to the firehouse to let him know I was onto him. He thinks *he's* a disrupter? Wait until tomorrow's picnic. This state doesn't belong to the billionaire class. People need to be woken up to what's going on. Tomorrow, I tell him I'm putting my foot down. Not in my backyard. No way."

I looked over the Maplewood Springs label. The first ingredient was high-fructose corn syrup. There was real Vermont maple syrup in there, far down on the ingredients list. This wasn't maple syrup; it was maple "product." MINO, we called it. "Maple In Name Only." The townspeople should have been rioting. Instead, they were slathering their pancakes with this junk.

They were under Jagger's spell. All morning, I'd thought the townies were pretending to be unimpressed by Bernie. They weren't pretending. They'd been bought and paid for by someone else. Joey said the tech CEO was throwing money around town. That must have been how my mother had upgraded to faster internet—I couldn't see it being viable for a private company or the state to snake gigabyte-level cables this far into the boonies. What was next, a sandy artificial beach? This was Eagle Creek, where beaches were made of rocks and mud. Like Mother Nature and the town founders intended.

Bernie pulled a steel flask from his jacket. "Maple syrup," he explained, dousing his short stack before passing the flask to me and Joey. "The good stuff."

As I was soaking my pancakes, Mayor Seeley approached the table. The sixty-something politico had what could only be described as a very tall head of hair. She traveled in a shroud of hairspray. She was as stuck in the eighties as my mother was stuck in the nineties.

"Mrs. Mayor," I said, quickly standing. "I'd like you to meet—"

She bumped me to the side with a sharp elbow and took over my spot on the bench. "Bernie, dear, it's been ages," she said, sidling up to him. "How are things in the swamp?"

"I'd shake your hand, but mine's covered in syrup."

"So's mine," she said with a smile.

Bernie harrumphed and returned to his pancakes. Thus ensued several seconds of awkward silence. When it was clear he wasn't going to engage with her, the mayor hopped to her feet and marched out of the firehouse. We ate in silence for several minutes, savoring the cinnamon and apple flavors in the pancakes, enhanced by the rich Vermont maple syrup Bernie had smuggled in. Doc had a knack for this sugaring business. I'd forgotten how good real maple syrup was.

"Sounds like you and Mayor Seeley have met," I said between bites.

"We were both on the Vermont mayors' council in the eighties. I remember one meeting, we just went at it. I was trying to convince her that capitalism was a failed system that oppressed the majority, but she wasn't having it. I'd never heard someone defend the honor of Milton Friedman with such passion."

"She's a force of nature," I said.

"That she is. We agreed to disagree. A lot. If somebody were to run against her, they'd have my endorsement in a heartbeat."

They'd have had my vote, too, if I'd still been an Eagle Creeker. She was the first and only mayor we'd ever had. Before her, our town had been so small that it could be run by a city clerk. A simple administrative position. But as the town's population grew in the latter half of the last century, so too did the need for bigger government. Prior to the first mayoral election in Eagle Creek, a goat had been serving as "honorary mayor." If you counted write-in votes, the goat would have beat Tamara Seeley in a landslide. Unfortunately, livestock is forbidden from holding public office in Eagle Creek according to the town's original charter. The goat died the following year and received a Viking funeral on the lake.

Was Mayor Seeley good for Eagle Creek? To paraphrase Bernie, a community is not judged by how many millionaires or billionaires it has, or by the size of the tax rebates handed out to greedy corporations. It is judged on how well it treats its most vulnerable citizens, and by the grade of its maple syrup. Using the latter measure, Eagle Creek was failing big-time.

As soon as Bernie finished his last stack, he signaled it was time to leave. Outside, side streets were being roped off for harvest festival vendors. If you were in the market for knitted winter wear, beaded necklaces, and framed photos of Lake Champlain, this would soon be your one-stop destination shop. As the sun set, downtown Eagle Creek would descend into absolute bedlam—one giant flannel-colored block party, fueled by light beer and jam bands. By nine, it would all be over for the day, because nobody went out after nine o'clock in Eagle Creek. Decent folk had no reason to set foot outdoors past that hour.

When we arrived back at the Eagle's Nest, Bernie retired to his room to work on his speech for the picnic. Joey said he had to leave soon, but followed me into the guest room. He wanted a quick peek around. The bed-and-breakfast had been the talk of the town when it had opened last year, but he'd never had a chance to check it out. His work took him all around the state, so he only got to Eagle Creek a couple of times a year. "Tyler did a great job remodeling in here," he said. "These wood floors are all new. What's your old room look like?"

"I don't want to know. I can only pray it's been aired out."

"You're the only person I've ever known who burned incense because they liked it, and not because they were trying to cover the smell of illicit drugs."

"I'd hardly call marijuana 'illicit,'" I said. "Isn't it legal in Vermont now?"

"There's a ban in Eagle Creek on growing cannabis within city limits," he said, picking up the mystery novel Bernie had lent me. "Same as in a lot of communities around here. Nobody wants to see maple syrup displaced as our number-one export. Although with the way that tech guy is buying up maple farms, I wonder how much longer we'll have a local economy. He doesn't hire people, you know. He hires robots."

"You don't have to pay robots minimum wage," I said. Had anyone started a robot union yet? It was either a brilliant idea or proof that I'd drifted so far to the left that I'd fallen into a political dead zone.

He received a text. "Good news," he said after reading it. "Well, for you, that is. They found Mr. Fletcher's boat crashed up on some rocks. Rhea closed the investigation. Accidental drowning. Doc's off the hook."

"Did anyone talk to him about it, or . . . ?"

"He wasn't home last night when I went 'round."

"So he won't know that I . . ."

Joey put a hand on my shoulder and looked me in the eye. "Don't beat yourself up. You did the right thing. It's over now, and we can put this behind us."

He finally left through the general store. I crashed facedown on the quilted bedspread and let my eyes close. The pancakes were finally catching up to me. A quick nap wouldn't be out of the question—in fact, I was owed a little rest and relaxation after my rude awakening this morning. Before sleep overtook me, however, there was a knock at the door.

"Mom?" I said, sitting up.

"It's Bernie," the senator said. "You weren't napping, were you?"

I roused myself from the bed and answered the door. Bernie was holding a manila envelope. "I could use a second set of eyes on something," he said. "If you're up to doing a little light reading."

"A speech?" I asked, taking the envelope. I peered into it warily.

He shook his head. "Somebody left this at my door, the one that leads to the back stairs."

For a split second, I thought it might be some *Watchtower* magazines. An overzealous Jehovah's Witness targeting bed-and-breakfast guests. A diabolical plan to convert us. They were going to have a hard time with Bernie, who'd been Jewish for eight decades.

What was inside wasn't a religious magazine.

I pulled out a paper-clipped sheaf of papers. It was a photocopy of Mr. Fletcher's autopsy report. It had been performed by the state medical examiner's office down in Burlington. The report was three pages, typed, with a predictably unintelligible signature. The filing date and time were yesterday, just before midnight.

Lana had warned me that constituents would try to hand things to Bernie. I was supposed to intercept them and, with a warm smile, let them know I'd hang on to their family recipe book/political manifesto/self-published mystery novel for the senator. Later, back at the office, I could make the determination whether it warranted the boss's attention . . . or deserved to be chucked into recycling. They'd gone straight around me, though, somehow sneaking up the back steps and correctly guessing which of the two rooms Bernie was staying in. I didn't like that. I didn't like that one bit. Still, it puzzled me why someone thought their state senator needed to see the autopsy of an accidental death. Did it have something to do with me finding the body?

PRELIMINARY FINDINGS:

   By report, 54-year-old deceased male found floating near the Eagle Creek marina docks in Lake Champlain. . . . Lack of diatoms in soft tissues (spleen, liver, kidney) and pleural cavity fluid rules out drowning in lake water as a cause of death. . . . Highly viscous liquid detritus occluding upper airway and trachea. . . .

Bernie was watching me read it in the doorway, his arms crossed. I double-checked the date of the autopsy. Something wasn't adding up. Joey would have mentioned this if he'd seen it. Right?

I skipped ahead to the last page. While there were enough fifty-cent words scattered throughout the rest of the report to fill out a year's worth of *Penny Saver* crosswords, the diagnosis was written in plain English.

PRELIMINARY DIAGNOSIS:

   Final diagnosis pending postmortem toxicology and lab results: Death by asphyxiation via choking on liquid detritus. Color and viscosity of detritus are consistent with processed xylem sap from the acer saccharum tree ("maple syrup").

"The case has already been closed," I said. "A drowning. Rhea said it was accidental."

"I love maple syrup more than anyone I know, but even I won't go for a swim in it. Who'd want to drown a banker in maple syrup?"

"Well . . ." I began then stopped.

"Well what? Tell me," Bernie said in that gruff commanding voice of his.

"Doc McGilliam?" I ventured.

"What? Doc McGilliam, the sugarmaker?"

"Doc had some beef with Mr. Fletcher, not sure what about. But it couldn't be Doc. Doc's an old hippie."

"So was Charlie Manson," Bernie said. He took the report from me. "I'm going for a walk. Need to stretch my legs after that breakfast. If you've got any clue what to make of this"—he raised the envelope theatrically—"grab your fleece jacket and join me."

"Sure thing," I said, still dazed from both being woken from my half-sleep and from the strange, shocking news in the report. "But first," I said, grabbing my key from the nightstand and yes, my fleece jacket, "coffee."

Chapter 9

Bernie wanted to soak up some of the atmosphere from the lake, so we walked out to the end of the second dock. The one where bodies didn't routinely float by. The other dock was open, though. No crime scene tape—that would have been too unsightly for the Champ Days crowds gathering across the way. Plus, I wasn't sure if the Eagle Creek sheriff's department even had yellow tape.

Although the air was cool, the sky was cloudless and the sun was out. A perfect autumn day in Vermont. Most of the boats usually docked here were out on the water. A steady stream of out-of-state cars were rolling through town now. Some were driving slower than the speed limit so they could take in the leaves, while others were driving slower, looking for parking for Champ Days. Most, presumably, hadn't heard about the dead man who'd floated to the surface less than sixteen hours ago.

"Did you know that Lake Champlain was one of the Great Lakes?" Bernie said. "For eighteen minutes."

"You're kidding."

"Blame President Clinton," Bernie said. "Actually, it was Pat Leahy who slipped the wording into a sea-grant bill. A little pork. Clinton didn't read it too closely, I guess, and neither did anyone else in either chamber. Took all of eighteen minutes for the *New York Times* to point it out and for the White House to overturn it." Bernie took a deep inhale. "Smells like a Great Lake to me. There was a nice breeze coming off the lake yesterday, but I couldn't get the window open. Last night was fine, but today it keeps getting hotter and hotter in there. If it's even one degree above sixty, I can't sleep. Can't do it."

"I'll talk to Mom," I said. I was just relieved Bernie hadn't wanted to meet out here because he was worried his room was bugged. This wasn't a meeting between two spies, although the manila folder in my right hand suggested it was more than a simple stroll for fresh air.

"Drowning pancakes in syrup is one thing," Bernie said. "But a person drowning in syrup? How does that happen?"

It would be weeks before either of us could eat a short stack with maple syrup without thinking of a dead man. Months, perhaps. Eating naked flapjacks was completely out of the question, of course. Without maple syrup, they're little more than corrugated cardboard Frisbees.

"What I want to know," Bernie said, "is how? And why? Whoever slipped this to me must have had the same questions, or else they would have given us more to go on."

Our Deep Throat's identity was a mystery. I'd snuck onto my mother's computer to check the security camera footage, but there wasn't any. The most recent recordings were from last night when Joey and I had met on the back steps. Whoever left us the manila folder had found a way around the motion sensors. A disturbing proposition.

Bernie and I had both read and reread the report. The medical examiner had laid out the facts, but the facts didn't give us all the answers. Mr. Fletcher didn't have anything else in his digestive tract besides maple syrup.

No pancakes.

No waffles.

Not even a spoonful of granola.

"You know what this looks like to me?" Bernie said. Then, without waiting for an answer: "A social media stunt gone wrong. One of those internet things, where kids are always doing dangerous stuff on video and ending up in emergency rooms. This Fletcher fellow chugs a gallon of maple syrup for the camera, chokes on it, and falls off his boat."

"Like a TikTok challenge," I said. "Although I'd imagine Joey or the sheriff's department went over all of Mr. Fletcher's social media accounts already. If he had any. That has to be standard procedure in cases like this."

"How much do you know about this Fletcher character?"

What I needed to do was get in touch with Joey. My phone was burning a hole in my jeans, but I left it untouched for the moment. I gave Bernie a quick rundown on Mr. Fletcher: Single. No kids. Lived alone. He'd been the bank manager at the Savings & Loan for seven or eight years. Prior to that, he'd worked at a national bank branch in Massachusetts. I'd had checking and savings accounts at Eagle Creek, but only interacted with the tellers. Online banking wasn't too popular in Eagle Creek. Vermonters valued that personal touch over cold, online chatbots. Although how much of an upgrade Mr. Fletcher was from a chatbot was debatable.

"Anything else?" Bernie asked. "You mentioned a dispute with Doc McGilliam."

He wasn't under any obligation to personally investigate the origins and validity of a document left at his door. He hadn't known Mr. Fletcher, as far as I could tell. He would have said something if he did. What was his interest in this case?

"I don't know what they were fighting about," I said. "Mr. Fletcher was the loan officer at the bank. He had the power to make or break a maple farm with the stroke of a pen."

"Bankers have never been well liked. Used to be anti-Semitism. Now, people's dislike of them is actually warranted. Blame Wall Street's pursuit of profits over people. The banks have cut a path of destruction through this country. 'Too big to fail' should be 'too big to exist.'"

"This is the Eagle Creek Savings & Loan. This is Main Street, USA."

Bernie rubbed his chin. "The amateur sleuth in the Cannon Cove books has a saying," he mused. "*This might be a small town, but there's no such thing as a small murder.*"

I almost choked on my own tongue. Neither of us had used the M-word, though surely it was on our minds. "We don't know he was murdered," I said. "He could have fallen into a barrel."

"You're talking about those fifty-five-gallon steel drums," Bernie said. "The ones that are three, four foot high. They look like big kegs, right?"

"Reserve barrels," I said. Every kid in Eagle Creek had taken at least half a dozen field trips to sugaring operations. If Bernie canned me, I could always become a maple syrup tour guide. "The bigger places stack them in warehouses, where they sit until they're ready to release the syrup into production. Maybe he was, I don't know, smuggling a barrel on his boat? And fell into it, choked to death, and landed with a splash in the lake."

"Sounds a little *Looney Tunes*, doesn't it?"

"I was bobbing for apples once in a trash can and lost my footing. Went straight in," I said. "Took three people to pull me out."

"Your folks must have been scared."

"Um, yeah." It had happened at a costume party last Halloween, but that was neither here nor there. "Back to the report," I said. "It did note in one of the subsections that there were traces of syrup in his nose, his ears, and even his hair."

"His hair," Bernie repeated. "If you're choking, how does it get in your hair?"

I thought back to Tyler last night, who'd greeted me with what I'd initially thought was maple syrup in his hair. Maple hair gel? Who in their right mind would use that? Maybe there was some sort of social media challenge making the rounds where people were dunking their heads into barrels of maple syrup.

The truth was, we would drive ourselves mad as two hatters going down various rabbit holes, trying to piece together a logical explanation for the strange details in the autopsy. Keeping Bernie on schedule this weekend was my number-one responsibility. The autopsy report was a wild card, a live grenade. As his acting personal aide, it was my job to jump on it and take the brunt of the blast. This was so far out of bounds, however, I worried that it might be time to loop Lana in. She could make the determination of whether we needed to call the fixer.

I ran through the conversation in my head:

This had better be good, she would say, slurring her words like she was two White Claws into the reception already.

It's not good. It's the opposite of good.

How bad are we talking?

There's a dead body—

Whose?

It's not important, I would say. *But someone's trying to rope Bernie into the investigation. I don't know who they are or what their angle is, but our boss has taken the bait. I didn't want to call the number you gave me, because it's not exactly life-or-death. Please don't fire me—*

I'm not firing you. You should call a moving truck, though, because you're being reassigned to the Sanders 2024 presidential campaign. Report to Des Moines on Monday.

Wait, he's running in 2024? I would ask, both thrilled to be privy to such closely guarded knowledge and slightly confused. To run for president as a Democrat—as he'd done twice before—he would need to primary the sitting president.

Lana would laugh. And laugh and laugh. And when she was done, she would laugh some more. *Of course I'm firing you. But you should look for work in Iowa anyway . . . because you'll never work in this town again.*

Yeah. Calling Lana was not an option. I was on my own here. But if I could handle it without Bernie getting his hands dirty, there was a good chance Lana would never need to know about it.

Whoever had leaked the report to Bernie had done so anonymously. They'd clearly wanted to go over the head of local law enforcement for some reason. Were they one of the other deputies, afraid to directly challenge Rhea because she was the sheriff's daughter? This being her first dead body, it could have been a simple error on her part. She might have gotten the autopsy report mixed up with another. Whatever the case, it was past time to call the professionals.

"Would you mind if I passed this along to Joey?" I asked. I was reasonably sure Joey wasn't our leaker. There was no reason for him to sneak the folder to the senator when he could have simply handed it to him at any point today.

"Go for it," Bernie said. The realization that this wasn't Cannon Cove must have finally dawned on him. With any luck, he would forget about it once the State Police were working on it and we could move on with our agenda. I hadn't racked up five years' worth of student debt at Georgetown to become an amateur gumshoe.

I texted Joey, asking if we could meet up somewhere in person. Cut down on the digital paper trail. I'd heard too many calls, text messages, and emails read aloud on the floor of the Senate. The fewer connections between the senator's office and a potential murder investigation, the better.

Joey had said there were a dozen murders in the entire state every year. Most, I assumed, were on the mean streets of Burlington (population: forty thousand). But this was Eagle Creek. A town that was becoming more and more of a tourist town every year, as leaf peepers pushed farther and farther north in search of fall color. Violent crime didn't happen here; it happened on the news. It happened in places like Burlington and Boston and, yes, the nation's capital. One murder and the leaf peepers would flock off. Instead of tourists, we'd be overrun with teenagers from surrounding counties trying to spook each other. *Beware the Maple Murderer of Eagle Creek . . .*

When Joey didn't respond immediately, we turned back to the store. On the surface, Eagle Creek was a postcard-perfect small town. It had all the pieces: a general store, a library, a town hall. A county sheriff's department to protect it all and keep order. There was comfort in the ordinary.

But there was nothing ordinary about Mr. Fletcher's death.

A gallon of maple syrup. That's the approximate amount the examiner had found, according to her measurements. She hadn't listed the grade, coloring, or viscosity. Being submerged in lake water for who-knew-how-long wasn't ideal for the preservation of evidence. The "further testing" alluded to in the report might clarify what kind of syrup we were dealing with. Either way, Doc was back on board as a suspect. Would he be back to haunt my dreams tonight? All that mattered to me, for the moment, was that I had the autopsy report in hand. Bernie could return to working on his speech for tomorrow's picnic.

Chapter 10

The general store was in disarray when Bernie and I returned. The pandemonium was as close to a prison riot as I'd ever seen. All five tables in the dining room were taken. A line stretching back to the ice-cream freezer had formed at the counter, all waiting on someone to come check them out. I could hear my mother in back, shouting at the grill. Never a good sign. Before I realized what I was doing, I had tied a store apron on out of instinct.

"Need a hand?" Bernie asked me.

I was supposed to be helping him this weekend, not the other way around. If anyone here got pushy with the senator, there wouldn't be any crowd control. On the other hand, turning him down would be rude. I told him I'd appreciate a hand, and he went table to table refilling coffees. This time nobody recognized him—he was moving too fast, a blur of white hair and long limbs.

I slipped behind the counter and started ringing the customers up. No one would look me in the eye. A few townies I recognized even glanced away, pretending not to know me. It wasn't because I hadn't shown my face in town for the past five years. Or not entirely because of that. I also had the taint of death on me. I wasn't just the prodigal daughter returned. I was bad luck.

"This line is ridiculous. No wonder this place is going out of business."

Maude Blooming. She had a multicolored, hand-knitted scarf wrapped around her neck. When she reached the counter, I put on my phoniest smile and thanked her for waiting. Like she had any choice. Where else in town could she get laundry detergent, a ham sandwich, and a bumper sticker that read WELCOME TO VERMONT. NOW LEAVE!

The line kept shrinking. I hadn't lost a step when it came to bagging groceries. The whole time, though, what Maude said continued to bug me. Sure, the store had seen better days. But there was a labor shortage; there were supply chain issues. Things everyone was dealing with lately. The loss of small farms was impacting the local economy, and my mother was undoubtedly feeling the trickle-down effects. But the store wasn't going out of business . . . was it?

There's a saying in customer service. *The customer is always right.* Anyone who's worked in retail for even a day can tell you this isn't true. Not even remotely. The customer always *thinks* they're right. There was another saying, one specific to Eagle Creek: *The Blooming sisters are always right.* Love them or hate them, Edwina and Maude had their fingers on the pulse. Even if they barely had a single pulse between the two of them.

When we were finished with the dinner rush, I took off the apron. There were only a few customers still in the dining area, chatting over coffees. Bernie had already gone upstairs to take a nap. There was a message from Joey on my phone. I hadn't felt the buzz, I'd been in such a zone.

I'm at the sheriff's right now finishing up paperwork. Here 'til 2 if you want to talk.

My mother put a hand on my shoulder. She thanked me for helping her. "You should head upstairs," she said. "You've got your own job. You don't need another. Tyler will be by soon."

Already twenty 'til two. I needed to head out now to reach the sheriff's department before Joey left. But I wasn't leaving without answers. I lowered my voice to a whisper. "Is the store in trouble?"

She sighed. "You have more important things to do this weekend."

"How long?" I asked. "How long do you have?"

"I can hold on two, three more months. Not through winter."

It was a punch to the gut. The store was all my mother had. It had been in the family three generations. She'd taken over right when it was about to go under, when it was deep in the red and my grandparents had passed in a car accident. A single parent with no alimony and practically no child support. Just a subprime loan that was still hanging over her head. The sweat, the tears, the sacrifices along the way . . .

"Is it the economy?" I asked her.

"Mostly. A lot of the sugarmakers who sold their farms to Maplewood have left town altogether. Every business in Eagle Creek has taken a hit. The B&B has helped make up for some of the lost sales. I think I could have weathered the storm, except . . ." She looked away, refusing to meet my eyes. "I put the store up as collateral for a loan. It was the only way Tyler could get his business off the ground."

"He couldn't get a loan by himself?" I asked. Tyler hadn't said anything, but of course local contractors had taken a hit. When money dried up, building projects were one of the first things to go. If I'd returned home more often, I might have known what was happening.

"Some of us need help," my mother said. "Let me rephrase that: all of us need help. Some of us ask for it."

I ignored her. "Have you tried talking to the bank? This isn't some big soulless corporate machine. This is Eagle Creek. You know everybody down there. There's, like, three people." I paused. "Two, now."

"I went down there and talked to Ferman last week," she said. "It was like talking to a brick wall. He said maybe we could 'work something out,' with this leering smirk. So I threw my drink in his face and left."

"What kind of drink was it?"

"Milk. Something was off about the taste, anyway. You can't trust those 'sell-by' dates on dairy products. Cows lie."

An image flashed in my mind of a darkened interview room, lit by a single, sad bulb dangling from the ceiling, the sheriff barking in her face: *Why'd you do it, Terri? Why did you kill Ferman Fletcher? Tell me, Terri . . . are you the Maple Murderer?!*

"He was a creep," she continued. "I don't know what he was suggesting, but I wanted no part of it. You'd have done the same thing. At least I hope so, if I raised you right."

"If you fall behind, banks have to give you time. I can't tell you how much of the senator's mail is from hardworking folks who are underwater. There's help available, if you know where to look. If you know the law."

She placed a hand gently on my cheek to rub a tear away. "I'm just glad you're home, Crash." She told me she'd get me the paperwork later in the weekend, if she could find it. I wouldn't have been surprised if the banker was also putting financial pressure on Doc. Their disagreement could very well have been about something more substantial than overdraft fees.

My mother wasn't a killer. She didn't have the strength to lift forty pounds, let alone a man of Mr. Fletcher's size. She couldn't unload shipments without Tyler's help. Besides, if she had even one murderous bone in her body, she would have used it to whack my father years ago. And he was alive and well, working at an alligator sanctuary in Florida last we'd heard. Three years ago, my mother had received an envelope with thirty-three dollars in cash for back child support. He'd included a note saying there had been more, but "the gators got his wallet." That was, presumably, why several of the bills were ripped up and taped back together.

On my way out of the store, I bumped into Tyler in the doorway. His head was freshly shaven. Before I could ask him why he'd buzzed his hair off, he was already past me. He'd not only avoided saying hello to me, he'd also acted like he hadn't even seen me. Had I done something wrong? Or could he sense I was becoming suspicious of him?

Because gentle giant though he was, I could see him doing something foolish when he'd heard the store was at risk of going under. If I was thinking it, then someone else would eventually think it, too. I could have ignored my straying thoughts if it weren't for one thing: Tyler's hair. He must have tried to wash it last night. When that failed, he had no choice but to shave it to get the stickiness out. The way he'd looked at his tacky fingers had told me he'd been as surprised to find it in his hair as I was to smell it. Maple hair gel? Or evidence of a crime?

Chapter 11

The sheriff's office was on the opposite side of town.

I made it there on foot in less than ten minutes.

Small towns for the win.

A Franklin County Sheriff's car was parked out front. I didn't see a State Police cruiser anywhere, but then I hadn't seen one back at the store this morning, either. Joey had said he'd already been in town when he got the call about Fletcher. I didn't know what he was driving these days. Not the rusted Tempo from our high school days if he had more than a dollar to his name. The steering wheel on that old beast shook so hard when you went over fifty-five that Joey once chipped a tooth.

The sheriff's office looked like a log cabin from the outside. Mainly because it was a log cabin. The thinking being, nobody on vacation wants to see a dull, gray concrete building with bars on the windows. Nobody wants to hear about murder, either.

When I entered, I found a half-full coffee, still warm, sitting on the front desk. No Joey. In fact, the other desks had been abandoned—some ages ago, from the looks of them. Desktops and filing cabinets were buried beneath towers of file folders. Even the five-foot, cross-eyed black bear that used to greet visitors was missing. Somebody must have realized what a total #taxidermyfail it was. The floor, meanwhile, had been converted into a nine-hole mini-golf course.

I called out for Joey. No answer. The only noise was the sound of Phil Collins singing in hushed tones that he could feel it in the air tonight (oh Lord), that he'd been waiting for this moment all his life (oh Lord). There was a silver bell on the front desk.

As soon as I dinged it, one of the side office doors flew open. Rhea poked her head out. She blinked hard a few times like she was waking from a catnap. I couldn't blame her. Their department was overworked—and, I would imagine, underpaid. The two usually went hand in hand. Bernie was one of the few members of Congress that seemed to even care about righting such wrongs.

"Don't scare me like that," Rhea snapped at me. She rested her hands on her belt, trying to muster up some fresh authority. The Phil Collins song was coming from inside her office. "That bell is for emergencies."

There was a pink stickie note underneath the bell, which I hadn't noticed. *RING BELL FOR EMERGENCY.* There were no instructions for what to do in the case of non-emergencies.

Phil Collins broke into his famous drum fill.

"My favorite part," Rhea said, playing air drums. "You know this song is about a drowning man. Phil Collins was watching his younger brother struggling to swim from a nearby cliff and couldn't reach him at the time. There was someone onshore, close enough to rescue Phil's brother, but they just stood there and watched. So he writes this song about it, and invites the guy to his concert—"

"—where he sings it to the guy, who has a spotlight on him the whole time," I said. "And then the guy is so ashamed he goes home and kills himself. Is that the story you heard?"

"All 'cept for the part about the guy killing himself. That's a tragedy all around."

"It would be, if any of it were true. The song's about his divorce. Phil's brother is still alive—he's a cartoonist."

"Is this what they teach in college? Kind of sad I didn't go, now."

I shook my head. "Looked it up on YouTube." I paused for a beat, not sure what else to say. "I actually came by to see Joey."

"You just missed him. Is there something I can help you with?"

Joey must have had to really run if he didn't even have time to text me. Such was the life of a big-shot detective with a fancy wide-brimmed hat. The autopsy report printout was folded into quarters in my jeans pocket. I considered showing it to Rhea. Would she see that she'd been wrong about Mr. Fletcher's manner of death, and reopen the case? Even if she did admit her error, she was bound to pop off at the whistleblower. The most obvious target would be Joey, because he and I were close. Or had been close, back in the day. If I told her the truth—that someone had slipped the report to the senator—that would create more problems, mainly for me.

That said, I couldn't afford to look a gift horse in the mouth. And I wasn't just saying that because Rhea had large teeth.

Although she did have quite the set of chompers.

"Speaking of drownings, I was going to ask him what was happening with the Ferman Fletcher case," I said. "I keep thinking about that poor man."

Rhea picked up a steel putter that was leaning against the front desk. She used it to retrieve a golf ball from under the desk. "Ain't nothing 'happening' with the case. It seems pretty straightforward." She lowered her voice. "Unless you've heard something otherwise?"

"I doubt I'd know more than you."

"Maybe there's some national security issue you're not telling me about," she said, putting the ball toward the closest hole, which—to my horror—was a black plastic rat trap. Her ball rolled over a rug and into the trap's pitch-black opening. "You forgot to tell me last night you were here with my favorite Vermont senator. Sad I couldn't make the event this morning."

"To be honest, I'd forgotten I was with Bernie last night. I was in shock. And no, there's no national security issue. If there was, I wouldn't have clearance anyway—I'm just an intern."

"That's no fun." Rhea shook the ball out of the trap and placed it back at the starting line. She handed me the club. "Your turn."

"If I'd known there was a mini-golf course here, I would have tried to get arrested in high school."

"There aren't any holes in the jail cell," she said.

I putted. My shot went wide. "Probably for the best."

The more we talked, the more I leaned into the idea that Rhea was clueless about the autopsy results. The entire department had a ramshackle feeling. The incompetence was astounding. Take the rat traps, for instance. If the bait was still in them, it meant there could be a rat lurking in any hole. We weren't playing mini-golf. We were playing rat roulette.

I tapped the ball. It went only a few inches. "What's the par on this hole?"

"You'd have to ask Dad. Sorry. 'Sheriff Kelly.' He set it up. He's really into golf." She used the toe of her boot to nudge the ball to a more favorable position for me. "He's playing with the big boys today."

"He's not working Champ Days?" I asked. Sheriff Kelly golfing on the town's biggest weekend of the year wasn't surprising. Sheriffs are elected officials. While their deputies take care of the actual work, sheriffs do what all elected officials do: spend an inordinate amount of time on golf courses.

"He's at a celebrity tournament down in Augusta. Left right after I closed the case. He'll be back on Tuesday."

"He's on vacation?"

"Everybody takes vacations, Crash. It's for charity. I mean, it's no Champ Days, but it's a big deal. They pair up police from around the country with celebrities. Most years it's not this weekend. Dad usually gets paired up with a local weatherman or radio DJ. Once, with the wrestler The Undertaker. This year, he'll be riding shotgun with Samuel L. Jackson."

Had the sheriff rushed his daughter to close the case, so he could get on the road? It was one thing to go knock out a few rounds after lunch on a Friday. But leave the sheriff's department flying rudderless during what was historically the busiest weekend of the year? This year, with a senator in town and a dead guy in the lake.

Then again: Sam Jackson.

The radio on her belt interrupted us with a squawk. After a quick back-and-forth through a staticky connection, Rhea holstered her radio. She flipped a sign around in the front door. *Back in 30 minutes,* it read. "Some kids are joyriding in a stolen golf cart. You remember those days, don'tcha? They're not going to get very far. Carl Withersby is chasing them on an ATV."

I walked with her to her car. "A friendly word of advice," she said. "Forget about Mr. Fletcher. You gave your statement. Don't let it spoil Champ Days for you." Then, as she was unlocking her police cruiser, she added, "If I don't see you again this weekend, it was great catching up. Tell your mother hi."

Seconds after she tore off down the highway, lights flashing, a familiar green Subaru pulled into the station's parking lot. The bass line of Jefferson Airplane's "White Rabbit" was thumping as hard as a Forester's factory system could thump. I only recognized the song because I'd had an *Alice in Wonderland* phase as a kid. A very intense *Alice in Wonderland* phase.

"Nice-looking cop shop," Bernie said. He had the windows rolled down. Either the wind had done a number on his hair or—just as likely—this was how he'd woken up from his afternoon nap. "You talk to your friend about the report?"

"He wasn't here. In fact, no one's here—Deputy Kelly just locked up for the day."

"You're kidding."

"Welcome to Eagle Creek."

He drummed his fingers on the steering wheel. "Need a ride back to the store?"

"It's a nice day. I can walk." I paused. Where was he on his way to? There weren't any events scheduled the rest of the day, of course. He was free to do whatever he wanted, even head back to Burlington for the night. It was preferable to having him wander around Eagle Creek by himself. Especially with the Maple Murderer out there. If anything happened to the senator, my career in politics would be over before it had even begun. Not even a letter of recommendation from Michelle Obama could help me then.

"Headed anywhere special?" I asked. "An apple orchard, a corn maze . . ."

He shrugged. "Thought I might check out the new Maplewood Springs sugar shack just outside of town, the one Wardlow invited me to have a look at. They do tours every hour. If we're lucky, he won't even be there."

"If you're looking for a shack with a tasting room, I can text my mother for recommendations. There have to be a few holdouts around here who haven't sold to Big Maple." I was specifically thinking of Doc, but there was a cloud of suspicion hanging over his head. Or there would be, once the investigation was reopened.

"If I was looking to do a tasting flight, I'd take you up on that offer," Bernie said. "Let me be frank: I might have a lead in this Fletcher case. I've got a hunch I want to check out."

"A hunch."

"You mentioned that Fletcher was the loan officer at the bank, which got me thinking. Who handled the farm buyouts for Maplewood Springs? Eagle Creek Savings & Loan. Fletcher knew where the bodies were buried. So to speak."

"What could you possibly hope to find there?"

"According to Maplewood's website, they have the largest climate-controlled maple syrup storage room this side of the border. With prices being what they are, I'm betting every other sugarmaker in the States shipped their last bottles months ago. So if one were to be submerged in enough maple syrup to drown . . ."

Lana hadn't prepared me for this. My boss had been reading too many mysteries. Now that he'd stumbled upon a real-life one, he was like a dog with a bone. Did dogs actually eat bones? I was a cat person. I had no idea what sick, twisted stuff dogs got up to in their free time.

Jagger Wardlow was living rent-free in Bernie's head. This was a personal fight for the senator. He wasn't going to let this go as easily as I'd hoped. I couldn't very well stop Bernie—we'd already established that. On the off-chance he was right, he would be walking straight into the snake's den. They'd almost collided like superpowers at the firemens' breakfast. There was no telling what Jagger Wardlow might do if Bernie started asking the wrong questions.

The smart thing to do would be to wait to hear from Joey.

This was no time for doing the smart thing.

"Unlock the door," I said, rounding the car. "I'm coming with."

Chapter 12

The turn-off for Maplewood Springs was a short three-minutes' drive from the edge of town. A small wooden sign on the roadside marked the sharp turn into the woods down a twisting one-lane gravel road, washed out and pitted in spots by rain and mud. If another car appeared around a curve, one of us would need to pull off the road to avoid a nasty collision. Ah, good ole backcountry driving.

"Just so you know," Bernie said, "this field trip is strictly off-the-clock. For both you and for me. The people of Vermont aren't paying us to poke our noses around a murder warehouse." He cleared his throat. "Excuse me. *Maple* warehouse. You're free to say no. I'm sure you have schoolwork?"

I flashed him the A-OK sign, which I only belatedly remembered had been recently co-opted by online white supremacists. Hopefully, Bernie didn't think I was some sort of secret Nazi. None of the racists I'd encountered over the years had been very secretive about their views.

"You said you talked to the deputy," he said. "She drop any clues?"

"Rhea's in over her head. I hate to say this, since I've known her since grade school, but I'd be surprised if she could solve Wordle in less than six guesses on a good day."

"What about the sheriff?"

"I'm not sure about his Wordle game."

"I meant what does he have to say about the case."

I explained the sheriff's whereabouts to Bernie as we crawled farther up into the hills. When I was finished, he let out a sigh. He didn't look surprised.

"Sam Jackson," he said. "He's got a handicap in the four–five range. Still, justice shouldn't have to wait until after the eighteenth hole." He drummed his fingers on the wheel. "I suppose you couldn't have just gone in there, waving the autopsy report in his face. It's his daughter who closed the investigation. That could be a tricky situation. Whoever leaked that report would find themselves in his crosshairs."

I snuck another look at my phone. Still no response to the follow-up text I'd sent Joey, letting him know I was heading to Maplewood Springs with the senator. The text said "delivered," but there was no indication he'd read it. There was a special circle in the underworld for people who didn't turn on their read receipts. It's a simple button in your phone's settings. It takes two seconds, people.

After ten long minutes of washed-out terrain, we crested a hill and pulled into a packed gravel lot. The maple trees surrounding the lot were a brilliant orange, putting on a real show for the leaf peepers hoping to check out some decent foliage. The sugar shack itself was a newly painted red barn several times the size of the average Vermont maple facility. Massive in scale, but tastefully country.

"Facilities like this used to be the size of a one-room cabin," Bernie said, pulling into the parking lot. It was packed with cars from around New England. "The sugar shack I converted in the sixties didn't even have electricity or running water."

The story about him and his first wife "going country" was central to the legend and lore of Bernie Sanders. I'd seen video of him talking about it, but this was the first time I'd heard it in person. Every time he repeated the story, it seemed like that poor shack in the woods was in worse shape. *No electricity or running water. Dirt floors. A bald eagle's nest in the rafters.*

Okay, I made the eagle part up. But would it have surprised anyone?

Land was cheap in Vermont in the sixties, and a wave of hippies, environmentalists, and independently minded folks of Bernie's generation were moving to the Green Mountain State. While Bernie and his wife weren't hippies, the "back to the land" movement clicked with the environmentalist couple. Their converted shack was modest—too modest, it turns out. Less than a year into their rural adventure, Bernie and his first wife moved back to civilization. Burlington was a town desperately in need of a progressive mayor to shake things up. The rest, as they say, is history.

We parked in the first open space, which was a good thirty yards from the shack at the end of the row of cars. About two dozen other vehicles sat in the lot. We wouldn't see any sap being boiled down into syrup. That only happened during the spring harvest. There was, however, the possibility of seeing some bottling in action. And where there was bottling, there were barrels. The kind you could cram a banker into.

"I'm going to ask some questions in there," Bernie said. "Watch and learn. Remember, I'm the head of the Senate Budget Committee. I've done this sort of thing a few times."

"You've used your position in the Senate to investigate suspicious deaths?"

"Corporate malfeasance, criminal negligence. Which, believe you me, can result in plenty of lost lives. More to the point, there's an art to wringing testimony out of a hostile witness."

I'd seen Bernie in action up close, grilling presidential cabinet nominees. "Art" wasn't exactly the word I would use to describe his technique, which ranged from barking to growling. Perhaps it was that Brooklyn accent of his. Either way, I wouldn't have wanted to be on the witness stand in front of him. Perhaps there was a method to his madness, after all.

We stepped out of the car. Bernie was locking up when a loud buzzing noise whooshed in above us. It sounded like a beehive was falling from the sky. Bernie ducked with the startled reflexes of a feral cat. Meanwhile, I was rooted in place, too spooked to move.

I shielded my eyes and looked into the bright sky. A backpack-sized drone was descending on us, its four helicopter blades a blur.

"It's a drone," I said. "No, wait—two drones."

A second had swung out from behind the first, and now they were both hovering in place above our heads, just out of reach. Was this the same pair I'd seen last night upon arriving in town? Had they been spying on us?

Bernie snuck a peek at them from his crouched position. "Are they looking at us?" he asked me. "Where are their eyeballs? Robots creep me out."

"Maybe you creep *us* out," a surprisingly human voice said from the drone on the left. There was a glowing red dot in the center of the front panel that pulsed when it spoke.

"Is someone in there?" Bernie shouted.

"Um, yeah," the drone replied. *"I'm* in here."

"Cut it out, Jerry," its pal said. "You're not going to win an argument with somebody who doesn't know basic robot anatomy. 'Where are my eyes?' Honestly."

Bernie turned to me. "I think this hunk of metal just insulted us."

Robot unionizing was now officially off my to-do list.

"Facial recognition and body temperature check is now complete," the one called Jerry said. "Please proceed to the entrance doors with your tickets ready."

Before either of us had a chance to respond, they shot straight up into the air like they'd been fired from a launch pad. I lost the drones in the sun but could hear them bickering back and forth. Within seconds, their voices and the buzzing of their blades were gone. The sky was clear again.

Bernie dusted his suit off. If my job was to aid the senator, I was failing. Good thing I wasn't technically his aide right now. "Off the books" didn't mean "stand back and do nothing," however.

"Do we have tickets?" I asked him.

"You mean, did I buy them online?" He shook his head. "I don't use my debit card on the internet."

I quickly looked up Maplewood's website and discovered they were, as I'd suspected, sold out the rest of the day. Of course they were. "I'm going inside to see if they have any cancellations," I told Bernie.

"I'm the lookout guy, then," he said. There was disappointment in his voice, like he'd just been told he couldn't have dessert until he finished his supper.

"I'll only be a minute," I said.

"Last time you said that, you were gone for forty-five minutes and found a dead body."

"If I find any bodies this time, I'm walking past."

Inside the lobby, there was a movie theater–style LED screen above an oak counter, another touch—like the drones—that ruined the rustic chic. It listed tour times for the rest of the day, every one of which was SOLD OUT. There wasn't anyone staffing the ticket counter to appeal to. It was all automated. No one's ever gotten far with the line, *I love that shirt, where'd you get it?* with a computer system. I couldn't even make a minor stink about the senator needing to go on a private tour. Not that I would ever pull the *Do you know who this is?* card. If word got back to Bernie that anyone was treating him like a celebrity, he'd blow a gasket. And he'd already blown a couple today.

Bernie burst into the lobby, flustered and out of breath. "Forgot to give you money for the tour," he told me, opening his wallet.

"They're sold out," I said. "It doesn't seem—"

A wooden barn door off to the side of the lobby slid open. We swiveled to see Jagger Wardlow standing tall at over six foot two, a thin smile on his lips. He was wearing a faded Nirvana concert tee he'd probably paid three hundred dollars for at a high-end resale shop. I wasn't about to flatter him for burning his money. At least he was wearing a shirt, unlike earlier.

"Welcome to Maplewood Springs," he said. "Welcome to Vermont 2.0."

Was he serious? I could taste the bile rising in my throat already.

"We don't need any fancy slogans," Bernie said. "All we need are two tickets for whatever the next tour time is."

"That would be Tuesday," Jagger said. "Could I interest you in a private tour instead?"

Bernie snorted. "Sounds expensive."

"While my time is extremely valuable, I would never charge the federal government for a private tour," Jagger said. "Let's call it an 'inspection.'"

Bernie snapped his wallet shut. "As long as we're clear there's no quid pro quo."

"Perfect. All I ask is that you keep your feet inside the marked walkway," Jagger advised us, leading us through the barn door. Another tour guide was taking a group room-to-room ahead of us. The group's chatter and laughter were in stark contrast to our "tour guide's" monotonous tech-speak delivery. "Disrupt this" and "pivot that" and "growth hack" everything else. He was less a person than the end result of capitalism run amok, a walking energy drink wearing a man suit.

Jagger did, however, have an eye for interior design. While the exterior of the building was classic Vermont, the inside was modern Dubai. It was divided into several large rooms, each with heavy machinery the likes of which I'd never seen in a sap processing facility. Everything was shut down for the weekend. "Some of these robots weigh over five tons. Accidents happen. Not here, of course. The laser-calibrated security system shuts everything down automatically if it detects an unauthorized incursion into the workspace."

I looked down. "If I stepped over the line painted on the floor . . ."

"Please, don't. The alarms are loud enough to wake the dead."

Interesting choice of phrase, I thought. But if security really was as tight as it appeared, the chances of Mr. Fletcher—or anyone on a tour—winding up inside a barrel around here by accident were minuscule. Even if he had died in an industrial accident, it didn't explain why I'd found him floating in the lake. If Bernie was looking for clues, he'd come to the wrong place.

"As you can see," Jagger explained, patting the side of a tall steel tank that reached into the rafters, "the evaporation tanks have been repurposed for the bottling process, allowing us to use the same basic components year-round. The entire production chain is vertically integrated. This allows us to keep it all in-house, from boiling the excess water to storing the syrup to eventually shipping to our distributors. This is innovation in action."

"All this machinery must eat up a lot of electricity," Bernie said. He didn't seem too impressed.

"Less than you might think. Certainly less than the old patchwork system. It's the efficiency of scale."

"The so-called patchwork system," Bernie said. "You mean the mom-and-pop farms. The little guys you've snapped up."

Jagger narrowed his eyes at us and stroked his chin. "The little guys were losing long before I'd even heard of Eagle Creek. More victims of climate change. Their way of life wasn't going to be viable much longer. Even by the science community's most conservative projections, Vermont maple syrup will be a thing of the past by the turn of the century. The clock is ticking."

He was right. I knew it. Bernie knew it. Maple trees only produce sap when the temperatures are below freezing at night and above freezing during the day. The Maple Belt was slowly shifting north due to the warming climate. By the end of the century, the hills around Eagle Creek would no longer be able to support the conditions necessary for sap production and we'd be eating our pancakes with Canadian syrup.

"Who maintains all of these robots?" Bernie asked. "You've got to have engineers, mechanics . . ."

"More robots," Jagger said.

"Who was the nut who programmed them? You must have some human beings around here, present company excluded. I need to pass along a complaint about those drones outside."

"Ah, my personal assistants," Jagger said. "Ben and Jerry. I wouldn't call them drones—not to their faces, anyway. They're touchy about terminology. They have the most advanced AI programming you'll find in use in the real world outside of the operating system running Mark Zuckerberg."

"Bah," Bernie said with a dismissive wave of his hand. "They're drones and they're jerks."

"Good help is so hard to find," Jagger said with his Tom Cruise smile.

The final stop on the tour was the climate-controlled storage room. Hundreds of fifty-five-gallon steel drums, just waiting until the market was right for them to be bottled. They were marked PROPERTY OF MAPLEWOOD SPRINGS and stacked on pallets floor to ceiling.

I patted one of the barrels as we passed through the room. The room temperature in here wasn't markedly different from the rest of the facility, but the steel drums were cool to the touch. "How long can you store syrup in here?" I asked.

"As long as we want," Jagger said. "Another flaw of the old system. A couple of bad years in a row can wipe out your average independent sugarmaker. We have the storage capability to hold on to product until market conditions are favorable."

"Huh," Bernie said, stuffing his hands in his pockets. "I thought it'd be bigger. Have you seen the National Reserve in Quebec?"

"I have," Jagger said in a clipped tone. "I can assure you, however, our production capability is light-years beyond that of any other US sugarmaker. This is just the tip of the iceberg. The underground storage is more than ten times . . ."

He continued to drone on, but I'd lost interest. Typical male. Insecure about his size.

Bernie finally cut him off. "You never answered the question I asked earlier," he said, crossing his arms. "I asked about the robots. Where do human beings enter the equation? Someone has to set up the miles of vinyl tubing in the hills around here, and maintain it when deer or squirrels get to it. You can't send a robot out there when there's snow on the ground."

"Ah, but we can," Jagger said. "All-terrain, subzero temperature-resistant units originally developed by NASA. The space program had a bit of a fire sale during the last round of government budget cuts."

"You don't have any shame, do you?" Bernie said.

Jagger arched an eyebrow. "My company is putting a lot of money into Eagle Creek and the surrounding area. It's a considerable investment. This entire weekend, in fact, wouldn't be happening without Maplewood Springs. The festival? It was broke before we stepped in. What have you done for Eagle Creek lately, Mr. Senator? Or, for that matter, for the state of Vermont?"

Bernie looked primed to explode.

We were back at the lobby. Our tour had come to an end.

"I'll see you at the parade," Jagger said, holding the door open for us, "Mr. Grand Marshal."

The tension in the air between the two was so thick you could spread it on a toasted bagel. Maplewood Springs's CEO obviously thought he was some sort of savior. That he was doing what was necessary to keep Eagle Creek afloat. The scary part was he might have been right. If Jagger Wardlow hadn't been the one to come gunning for the maple industry, someone else eventually would have. A private equity firm, a hedge fund. The industry's reliance on hobbyists and micro-farming techniques had made it a sitting duck. Now Farmer Bro was here to turn it all around. That didn't mean he had to rub his superiority in everyone's face. It was easy to see why he was so hated online. There was a bounty on his beard—$455,000 US, payable in Bitcoin.

Did I mention he was only a year older than me?

I'd never wished harder in my life for a pair of scissors.

Chapter 13

As we returned to the car, I scanned the skies for Ben and Jerry. No sign of Jagger's personal drones. "So what do you think?" I asked Bernie.

"He talks a good game. It all sounds rehearsed."

"He must have given this same tour to other VIP guests," I said.

Bernie found his keys. "You think?"

"He's probably more comfortable talking microchips than maple, but I—"

Bernie stopped while opening his car door. "Do you hear someone shouting?"

I didn't hear anything, other than the sound of a chainsaw. "I hear someone cutting up firewood. That's it. You hear that a lot around—"

I couldn't get out the rest of my sentence because Bernie was already heading into the woods. "Senator!" I yelled, rushing to catch up with him. Lana hadn't been kidding about his speed. I found him standing by a tree, not even out of breath. The man didn't know the meaning of "slow down." In life, and in politics. He wouldn't retire; he would be dragged kicking and screaming from office. And then what? I couldn't imagine him sitting around in God's Waiting Room watching *Celebrity Jeopardy!* and eating mashed potatoes.

"Look at all of these sugar maples," Bernie said, shaking his head. "I remember when sugarmakers used to hand-tap trees and trek their bounty in metal buckets up and down the hills to the sugar shacks. Takes moxie to work these hills."

"I've never been that outdoorsy," I said.

"Blue-collar workers are the heart of this country," he said. "I was a carpenter for about six seconds when I first moved to Vermont. Didn't take me long to realize that I didn't have the hand-eye coordination required for power tools. Last time I used a hammer, I wound up with the cuff of my sleeve nailed to our living room wall. Jane changes the lightbulbs now."

"Why were you using a hammer to change a lightbulb?"

"That's what Jane asked, too."

This explained the memo about never letting Bernie change a lightbulb in the office. His chief of staff wasn't trying to prevent him from getting his hands dirty—she was trying to prevent him from getting electrocuted.

We walked on until we reached a clearing, where a crew of timber workers were cutting up a felled tree. There were three workers with hard hats and goggles hacking away at a thick trunk. It wasn't an injured tree that they were working on. Far from it. It was a majestic maple whose orange leaves would never get to fall as they should. There were several dozen stumps in the area.

Bernie marched across the clearing to confront the workers. I followed, but couldn't hear what he was shouting at them.

His words were being drowned out by the roar of the chainsaws. As a general rule, I tried to avoid yelling at anyone wielding power tools.

When the loggers saw him approaching, they stopped working. One of them—a woman I recognized but couldn't place—told the others to take five. She removed her safety glasses. It was the *Larry Sanders Show* fan from the store. Her wolf-cut was now tied up with a red handkerchief. I looked down and, yes, she still had her muddy boots on. They were twice as muddy now.

"—some nerve cutting good wood like this," Bernie said, still shouting despite the chainsaws having quieted. "These are old-growth sugar maples."

Muddy Boots was unmoved. "We're already a day behind because of what those kids did the other night. Any further disruptions, and it's going to come out of my own pocket. So forgive me if I don't have much patience, but we need to get back to work."

"Are you union?" asked Bernie.

She laughed and turned to her co-workers, who were sitting on tree stumps. They were going to have sticky bottoms the rest of the day. "Hey, guys. Larry Sanders's brother is going to tattle on us."

"These are healthy trees," Bernie protested. "You need a thousand different permits to cut down a tree in Vermont!"

"This is private land," another of the workers said. "And I've got your permit right . . . here." I'm not going to describe the gesture he made toward the senator, but suffice to say it would have led to censure had it occurred on the Senate floor.

"Hey, let's take it down a notch," Muddy Boots warned the man.

He sheepishly put his hands in his pockets. "Sorry, boss."

"Could we ask who owns this land?" I said, stepping in before Bernie re-escalated. "If there's some sort of mistake, we'll take it up with them. I'm assuming it's Maplewood Springs."

"What do you think?" Muddy Boots asked. A rhetorical question. "Listen. We've had some trouble at this worksite. Someone filled a tractor's gas tank with syrup the other night. Total loss. Pretty expensive prank, if you ask me. Cost us an entire day's work as well. That's why we're here on a Saturday. You think I don't want to be with my kids down at Champ Days?"

Jagger Wardlow hadn't mentioned any trouble on his land when we'd spoken to him. Who would sabotage a worksite this deep into the hills? There were easier targets for vandalism. My money was on protestors. On the surface, the townspeople appeared to be united in thinking Maplewood Springs was the best thing to happen to Eagle Creek since indoor plumbing. Was there an underground resistance to Big Maple that neither Bernie nor I knew about? Surely not everyone had folded the moment Jagger Wardlow's boat docked in town. Doc McGilliam hadn't sold his farm, as far as I knew. There could be other holdouts as well.

Why buy hillside farmland like this and then remove your cash cow? Jagger hadn't said a word about a new storage or processing facility. Had Jagger found a way to make more money with the land than sugaring? A luxury hotel, perhaps? He'd have a hard time filling it in the winter months, since Eagle Creek was a long way from the popular skiing destinations. The ice fishers who came up this way wouldn't pay luxury prices. It sounded like a fool's errand. Jagger Wardlow, while many things, had never struck me as a fool. He was, as we said in Vermont, clever as a Yankee.

As we returned to Bernie's car, I could have sworn I heard the trees screaming as the chainsaws started up again.

Chapter 14

After our trip to Maplewood Springs, we returned to town. To cheer Bernie up, I took him to the Blooming sisters' gift shop on the square. They sold every kind of maple syrup and maple syrup product you could think of, and quite a few you couldn't. A steady stream of foot traffic passed in and out of the shop as we were browsing.

"When I first moved to Vermont, we had syrup—that was it. Maple syrup," Bernie said, wandering through the gift shop. "It was dark as night. Tasted like it, too. We used to swig it straight from the bottle. Had a real kick. The guys on third shift over at the paper mill drank it to stay awake. I never liked the stuff. The light stuff—that's more my speed."

The market for maple products had exploded in the past several years. Even Starbucks had introduced a maple-flavored fall drink (forget, for the moment, that sap is harvested in late winter and spring). The sheer number of products in Everything's Maple was mind-blowing. I was searching for a very specific type of maple syrup product, however: hair gel.

Bernie picked up a tall pink beer bottle. "Voodoo Doughnut Bacon Maple Ale," he said, reading the label. "Bet that has a kick."

"We could open a bottle and find out," a heavyset woman said from the next aisle. "I'm sure the sisters wouldn't mind."

It was Mrs. Bowers, my school bus driver from elementary through junior high. She had ruled the bus with a stern but fair hand, and often surprised us with home-baked goods. Her maple pecan cookies were the best I'd ever tasted.

"You still driving the school bus?" I asked.

"Glaucoma," she said. "Forced retirement. I'm getting surgery next year. It's been a change of pace, not having to deal with a bunch of screaming brats pawing and clawing at each other. No offense, of course."

"Brats" was one of her many terms of endearment for the kids she drove. Other names she'd used to describe her bus riders over the years included monsters, trolls, critters, mutants, and—my personal favorite—ankle biters.

Bernie set the beer back on the shelf and held his hand out to my former bus driver. "Bernie Sanders," he said.

"Dina Bowers," she said, clasping his hand in her palms like it was a frog she'd trapped. "I've got to tell you, the maple-flavored Bernie hot sauce they carry here is to die for."

She didn't let go of him. I'd seen this a couple of times today already. Vacationing flatlanders so starstruck they forgot they were still holding hands with the senator. Mrs. Bowers might have been a local, but she had no shame when it came to showing her affection for Bernie. Only one way to break her hold.

I accidentally-on-purpose bumped a display of soap, knocking several bars to the floor. It startled her out of her trance, allowing Bernie to escape her clutches. I picked the soap up and began placing it back on the display.

"Maple syrup soap?" Bernie said, picking a bar up.

"It's not my favorite," Mrs. Bowers admitted in a hushed voice. "The sisters swear by it, though."

Maude poked her head out of the storeroom. "What is going on out there? Edwina?"

"She stepped out for a minute," Mrs. Bowers shot back.

This didn't sit right with Maude, who swore under her breath and joined us in scooping up the soap. "Someone needs to keep an eye on these tourists," she whispered. "Else they're liable to walk off with half the store."

"Who will peep the leaf peepers?" I said in a lofty voice, to the amusement of exactly no one. I cleared my throat and turned to Maude. "Do you have any maple hair products?"

She laughed. "The one shampoo we had in here had the consistency of syrup. It wasn't sticky, but you can imagine somebody pouring that onto a waffle and—bam!—lawsuit. We stopped carrying it."

"I was looking for hair gel."

"Can't remember ever seeing that around here. Sorry."

Bernie took a tentative sniff at one of the bars of soap. He jerked back from it, like a wasp had flown out of it and up his nose. "Any bottles of the hot sauce left?"

"We keep it behind the counter—it's that popular," Maude said. She fetched a bottle for Bernie. It wasn't just any old hot sauce; it was maple sriracha. There was a cartoon illustration of Bernie's head with flames shooting out of his mouth and ears. FEEL THE BERN! the label promised. A bold claim. Surprisingly, Bernie was taking this in stride . . . until he turned the bottle around and saw the bottler's name.

"A *Maplewood Springs* product," he read out loud, his face growing red as the sriracha. "Hmm."

"They have a sugar shack just outside of town," Mrs. Bowers piped up. When she caught sight of the look on Bernie's face, she quietly backed off, returning to her own shopping.

Maude told Bernie he didn't have to pay for the hot sauce, but he insisted. They went back and forth a few times, and she finally relented. "Then I'm ringing you up with my employee discount," she said. "Fifteen percent off, and that's final."

Maude rang my maple-scented sunscreen up at full price.

As Bernie and I were returning to the Vermont Country Shed, I asked him about the unlicensed hot sauce. "Are you taking that to a lawyer?"

"I'm taking it to Jane," he said. "I don't give gifts to lawyers."

"I meant them using your likeness," I said. "I'm assuming you didn't grant anyone—especially Farmer Bro—permission to make Bernie hot sauce."

"If I sued everyone who used my face to sell their junk, I wouldn't have any time for legislating," he said. "There are Bernie T-shirts, Bernie coloring books, Bernie action figures. Those Flunko Plops are the worst. They made my damn head too big. I look like one of those Precious Moments dolls from the eighties."

The only thing I'd bought inside was the travel tube of sunscreen. My skin was so fair, I was liable to burn if the moon was full. "Want some?" I asked, squirting a splotch into my hand. It was the color of brown mustard. As I massaged it into my forearms, it went on clear.

Bernie shook his head. Sunscreen was already part of his morning skincare routine, he explained. "When you start thinning upstairs, you don't have any choice. Plus, I'm not sure I want to smell like maple syrup all day. I'm worried it would make me hungry at odd times."

The sunscreen had a sweet smell, but wasn't at all sticky. "Ten years ago, they didn't have much besides syrup," I said.

"And now they've got every darn maple product you can imagine," Bernie said. "Except for one."

Maple hair gel, I thought.

"Not a single bottle of Grade A Golden," he said.

My mother hadn't been exaggerating. "It was a brutal spring."

"That it was," Bernie said. "And did you notice half the stuff in there was Maplewood Springs this, Maplewood Springs that. Wardlow has his claws sunk deep into Eagle Creek. Is there anyone who isn't in his pocket? If he was involved in a crime—let's say, hypothetically, murder—who's to say he doesn't already have the sheriff on his payroll?"

"I don't know."

"He's not content with owning Eagle Creek," he said. "He's building something up in those hills—a large-scale processing or distribution center, is my guess. I've been using the phrase 'Big Maple' to wake people up to the threat he poses. If he continues on this path, Wardlow will make it reality. There's no need to expand, but that's never stopped some corporate suit. It's the same story. It keeps repeating itself. When is enough *enough* for these people? Eighty percent of all income goes to the top one percent. And yet they need more. Fifty million is not enough; they need one hundred million. One hundred million is not enough; they need one billion. When will it stop?"

"At murder?"

"He wouldn't have done the deed himself," Bernie said. "Most of these billionaire types pay someone else to do their dirty work. If your average Joe Lunchbucket can hire a hit man for four or five grand in Cedar Rapids, Iowa, imagine how easy it is for someone like Jagger Wardlow."

Why had someone chosen this weekend, of all weekends, to take Mr. Fletcher out? The same weekend that Jagger Wardlow was in town. Last I'd heard, the tech CEO lived in Texas. Sure, maybe he had multiple homes around the country—and around the world, and probably on the International Space Station—but the chances of him being here in Vermont, simultaneous to Mr. Fletcher's death and Bernie's appearance . . . I didn't buy it. And neither did Bernie.

"Mark my words: Wardlow's got blood on his hands," Bernie said. "Blood and sap."

Chapter 15

"Thirty million Americans make minimum wage," Bernie was saying. "Let's call it what it is: a starvation wage. In Vermont, we've raised the minimum wage five dollars in the past five years, and it's still not enough. What we need is a fifteen-dollar minimum wage—not just in this state, but in every state in the union.

"Raising the minimum wage would benefit women, who are disproportionately forced into low-paying jobs. It would benefit African Americans and Latinos, who are likewise disproportionately represented in the low-income bracket."

Bernie was on a roll, but he wasn't done yet.

"This is not some radical idea. This is not some liberal pipe dream. Voters in Florida—a state that Donald Trump won, let me remind you—approved an increase to the minimum wage through a ballot initiative by a huge margin. It is an absolute imperative that Washington listens to the people of this country.

"The House has already done their part. Now the Senate needs to pick up the ball and run with it. I'm calling on my colleagues to pass legislation raising the federal minimum wage to fifteen dollars an hour. Let us go forward together into a better tomorrow."

For seven long seconds, Bernie's words hung in the air. He'd nailed every beat, every applause line. No teleprompter. No legal pad.

There was only one problem.

"Sir, this is a food truck."

The teenaged girl working the tablet computer in the window was nonplussed by Bernie's diatribe. He'd asked her if the owner of Paglio's Poutine paid her a decent wage. She had made the mistake of telling him her hourly wage—more than her friends made at their part-time summer jobs, but nothing close to fifteen dollars an hour even with tips.

We carried our food to a folding table in the street. Downtown was roped off for the night's festivities. Two dozen townspeople and a handful of tourists were already milling about. The first band would begin playing in the library parking lot soon, at five. Then things would get wild. Nice weather and the promise of more free Maplewood Springs hoodies meant Champ Days was expecting more than five hundred people a day this year.

Bernie set his paper plate of poutine on the table with a wet thump. It was the tallest single serving of fries, cheese curds, and gravy I'd ever seen. No wonder it had cost thirty bucks and required a signed health waiver.

"These fries are cold," Bernie said, chewing with a full mouth. The fries had been removed from the fryer fifteen minutes ago, well before he'd decided to use the concrete outside the food truck as an impromptu political rally.

"Used to be, if you wanted real poutine, you had to go to Canada," Bernie said. "I usually eat at roadside diners on the road.

Easier to eat healthy—I'm not supposed to have this stuff, after that heart business. Sometimes, though, it feels good to be bad."

I'd opted for a shake, and had, predictably, slurped it down too fast. An ice cream headache had taken ahold of my frontal lobes. As I rubbed my temples, I considered a little hair of the dog treatment—a chocolate soft-serve cone chaser, maybe.

"Where's Champ?" Bernie asked.

"You mean the lake monster?" I said. "In the lake, I guess. If you believe in that sort of thing."

"You don't?"

I stared at him, trying to figure out if this was a test of some sort. I decided to proceed with caution. "I'm not going to deny there are stories of sea serpents around here dating back to the Abenaki. They called it *Gitaskog*. 'The Great Snake.' Anyone who's ever spent time on the lake has tales."

"I'm sensing a 'but' . . . "

"Plesiosaurs went extinct sixty-five million years ago," I said. "The lake is around ten thousand years old. The math doesn't add up."

Bernie shrugged. "Maybe you're right. It might just be some fish story, but the festival's named after him," he said, waving his hands around in little circles. "Where are the Champ toys? If I was a kid expecting to see a lake monster, I'd throw a tantrum. All you've got is that statue out at the marina, although it looks a little more like a brontosaurus than a lake monster."

"It's an old Sinclair gas station dinosaur," I said. "But yeah. 'Champ Days' is just the festival's name. I think 'Maple Days' was taken, so, y'know, next best thing. There's a Champ float in the parade. You won't be able to miss it, because you'll be on it. That's one of the benefits of being grand marshal. I wasn't sure if you, uh, knew about Champ."

"Big green fella, long neck, flippers?" Bernie said, stretching his arms and flapping them. "Champ is the mascot of Burlington's collegiate baseball team. Where I have lived for many, many years. You're not secretly a flatlander, are you?"

My face flushed with embarrassment. "I was born in Vermont, trust me. I'm just not big into sports."

"Baseball's more than a sport," he said. "It's America's pastime. Next time you're in Burlington, let me know. I've got box seats. First base line. There's even a net, now, so fly balls won't bounce off your face." He wiped the final traces of gravy off his plate with his last, cold, soggy fry. "What's on tap tonight?"

"It's quarter to five," I said, reading the tall clock in the town square just over his shoulder. "Your schedule is free until tomorrow."

"If you want to head back to the B&B, go ahead. I need to let this poutine settle."

Leave him here by himself? I wasn't babysitting him, I reminded myself. And the band was doing soundcheck and sounded pretty good. And if I'd learned anything over the past twenty-four-odd hours, it was that there was only one person in Bernie Club: Bernie. Bernie was going to do what Bernie was going to do. That didn't mean I couldn't steer him in a slightly less conspicuous direction.

"Don't take this the wrong way, Senator, but you were starting to draw a crowd back there, talking about minimum wage. Despite the turnout at this morning's event, you're not exactly flying under the radar." I was hoping he would head inside when I did.

"Can I help it if people are drawn to my ideas?"

My phone interrupted us. It was Joey, finally getting back to me. He'd had to run home to his parents' for a minor family emergency, and had just now seen that I'd been trying to reach him all afternoon. He sounded like he was out of breath.

"Everything okay with your folks?" I asked.

"It's my sister," he said. "She's twelve now. The last year she's eligible for the Maple Queen contest. My parents don't want her doing it—"

"Because it's ridiculous, dated, and sexist?"

"That doesn't bother them. It's the speech portion. She wants to give a TED Talk on cryptocurrency. Apparently, she has a slideshow and everything." He groaned. "I looked it over—it all went over my head. Then I find out my parents have been paying her allowance in something called 'Dogecoin' and I just . . ."

"You need a drink?"

"You're speaking my language, Crash."

We agreed to meet at the Moose Knuckle in twenty. I asked Bernie if he needed me to do anything more this evening. The particulars of tomorrow's picnic had already been set up by the district office. The local volunteers were driving up from Waterbury, which wasn't far from Burlington. We were all meeting at eleven at Ebenezer Allen High. The picnic would begin at one with a speech from Bernie.

"You kids go have fun," he said. "I've got some digging around to do tonight."

"Digging? Digging what? Please tell me you're starting a winter garden."

"Just digging up what needs digging up. But I'll keep a low profile—scout's honor."

"Senator—"

He waved his hand, shooing me away. "I know what I'm doing. I've read every *Cannabis Beach* novel—except the most recent. My neighbors really need to read faster."

My ice cream headache had turned into a political headache. I'd gone along with Bernie's plan to investigate the Big Maple angle. As a person, I appreciated that a politician actually cared about the death of a constituent who—let's be honest—likely hadn't voted for him. As his intern who really, really didn't want to get fired, I would have preferred he left the sleuthing to the police.

Plowing through a seventeen-book series about an edible baking amateur sleuth? That was one thing. The worst that could happen was a paper cut or giving yourself a black eye when you dropped your e-reader on your face. This wasn't a mystery novel, however. If Bernie dug too deep, his biography might end up getting shelved in bookstores under "true crime."

Chapter 16

Joey flipped back and forth through the autopsy report trying to make sense of it. We were sitting at a table under the Moose Knuckle's straw awning, sipping our drinks. The real action in town was underneath the Champ Days beer tent. We had the Moose mostly to ourselves, which was one reason I'd wanted to meet here. The brewery had been a tiki bar once upon a time. They still had piña colada on tap, which was another reason I'd asked Joey to meet here.

"Maple syrup," he said. "You're sure this report isn't a prank?"

"If it is, someone's got a twisted sense of humor."

"One phone call down to the state medical examiner's office would clear it up," Joey said. "Trouble is, the office isn't open on the weekends. Could take some time to track the M.E. down. Do you recognize any of these medical terms? You're in a science program."

"I'm in a political science program, which isn't the same thing. But I googled the stuff I couldn't decipher. He didn't just choke on syrup, he drowned in it. They found it in his lungs. His ears. *Everywhere.*"

Joey raised an eyebrow. "Even down there?"

"Mind out of the gutter," I said. "Everywhere above his waist, I meant."

He shuddered. "Must have been one big bottle."

"I'm thinking it was a barrel," I said. "And this time of year? There's only one place that has maple syrup barrels lying around."

"Maplewood Springs," he said. "Have you looked at your mom's security footage yet, to see who might have leaked this to you?"

"There are cameras on every door, but there's no footage from this afternoon. The camera was supposed to automatically turn on. Either it's defective, or someone found a way around the security system."

He folded the papers. A light breeze was passing through the open-air bar. Portable gas heaters were set up around the Moose, though none were yet turned on. The night was young.

"Look, Crash, I appreciate you bringing this to me. If it's legit . . ." He paused. "Let me worry about this, okay? You're off the hook."

Except I wasn't. There was Doc, and there was my cousin. "Can I tell you something? Promise you won't get mad."

"You've been working on a list of suspects."

I buried my face in my hands, but peeked out between my fingers.

He was grinning. "I know how your mind works. Remember when I came out to you, and you made a list of guys to set me up with?"

Oh God. I'd written down half the boys' names in our high school. All of whom were straight. My matchmaking skills were—and remain—poorly calibrated.

"It's not like that," I said, letting him know I was serious. I told him about the dispute between my mother and the bank, and that I was worried my cousin might be involved in some way. Saying it out loud, it was almost silly.

"If word gets out that this wasn't an accident, there's going to be a lot of finger-pointing around here," Joey said. "Not saying you don't have reason to be concerned about anyone suspecting Tyler, but he's not the only one in town to end up on the wrong end of a bank loan. First thing I need to do is see if whoever leaked this to Bernie also leaked it to Burlington. I'll need some additional boots on the ground, anyway. The sheriff's department has their hands full with Champ Days."

"And golfing with Nick Fury."

He rolled his eyes so far back they were almost completely white. "These guys. I swear. If I were mayor, I'd ask for Sheriff Kelly's resignation on my desk first thing Monday morning."

"It's a holiday," I pointed out.

"Then Tuesday morning," he said. "If you'll excuse me, I need to make a couple of calls."

I watched him duck out into the parking lot, phone to his ear. While he was gone, I checked my phone. There was a text from Bernie.

Nobody's seen Doc McGilliam since last night.

Was he interviewing witnesses, now? So much for keeping a low profile. With one swallow, I finished off Joey's piña colada.

Joey wasn't gone long. He returned with a water—a bad sign.

"Something's the matter," I said.

"Exactly. Looks like I'm the only detective in this state who's not kneeling to the porcelain god right now," he said. "The entire department went out to eat yesterday at the Appaloosan Buffet."

"Let me guess—they ordered the crab-stuffed lobster?"

"How'd you know?"

I told him about the district office being wiped out by the very same entrée.

"We've got another problem, too," I said. I relayed Bernie's message about Doc. "So what do we do?"

"Nothing," he said. "Doc's allowed to get out of town if he wants to. He's not a suspect. And I'm going to let the mayor know about this, but—based on my experience—I don't think there's a public danger. This has all the hallmarks of a revenge killing. Even if it was random, it's Champ Days. I already know what the mayor's going to say: the show must go on." He forced a smile. "It's going to take some time to officially reopen the investigation. I don't want to publicly embarrass Rhea—she may not have seen this report," Joey said. "If you could keep a lid on what's in this report until it's public knowledge . . ."

"I've already posted my first podcast on the Maple Murderer. Should I take it down?"

He stared at me. "I can't tell if you're joking."

"Joey, when would I have time to record a podcast? My lips are sealed."

"Good, good," he said as he stood up and dropped some money on the table for a tip. "Thank Bernie for me. Let him know what's left of the Vermont State Police are on the case."

I should have felt better. Why, then, did I feel like I'd just dragged Joey into something that could go sideways at any point? I had just pawned off the investigation to my former bestie. *As you should*, I reminded myself. *That's his job, not yours.*

Since we didn't have anything on the schedule for the rest of the evening, I decided to head back downtown to Champ Days. The party would go on a few more hours. I didn't know who I'd run into—old friends, old enemies. Old frenemies. Maybe I'd see if they were serving up cider in the beer garden. I returned to my room to grab my fleece. The temperature was plummeting now that the sun had set.

The light was on under Bernie's door. He was watching CNN on his iPad. Probably out of the corner of his eye while he worked. I'd heard enough stories of him trashing drafts the night before a big speech and starting from scratch. He would be up late into the night, I guessed, making notes on his yellow legal pad.

I decided not to head back out tonight. While it would have been fun for old times' sake, I had work to do, too. And by the time I finished my write-up on Bernie's "meet the people" disaster and emailed it to Lana, it was past eight. Less than an hour until Champ Days wound down for the evening. Even if I was back in DC, I still would have turned in for the night. This wasn't undergrad any longer. When I had more than two drinks these days, I felt it in the morning. That was not something I needed this weekend. I changed into my PJs and got under the covers. It was time to see what was happening in Cannon Cove.

Interlude

Mary-Jane was in the kitchen of her tiny bakeshop when the bell above the front door jangled. She was waiting for her young assistant, Bud Majors. He was supposed to have opened up today but was MIA. She'd texted him twice, but he hadn't responded. She'd hired him as much for his shaggy, bleached-blond hair as for his baking skills. Her clientele loved him . . . and his patented "special" brownies.

"I'll be right there," she yelled, removing her gloves. When she pushed through the kitchen doors and saw who it was, her heart skipped a beat. It wasn't Bud Majors.

"Mike," she said, shocked to see the sheriff out of uniform. "What are you doing in town? Shouldn't you be—"

"—in Key West?" He smiled that crooked smile of his. "It wasn't the same without you."

This man was trouble with a capital T. Mike was charged with keeping law and order in Cannon Cove. She was the town's resident amateur sleuth, sticking her nose where it didn't belong. While he'd tried warning her away from his murder investigations at first, Mike had come to appreciate the unique perspective she brought to the table. Mary-Jane helped him solve dozens of cases with her encyclopedic knowledge of the works of Agatha Christie.

Their flirting never went anywhere, however. Even a trip together to the National Sheriffs' Conference in Key West last winter hadn't resulted in anything, other than them solving a murder in their hotel. This morning, though, things felt different between them. Her breath quickened . . .

The door flew open. It was Mary-Jane's mother. She always had a knack for showing up at the worst possible time. She was supposed to be a silent partner in Mary-Jane's business, but she was in and out of the bakeshop so much she might as well have been drawing a paycheck. This morning, she was in a red kimono. Her equally red hair was drawn up into a bun.

"Hello, Mrs. Taylor," Mike said. "I was just on my way out."

Mary-Jane's mother threw her hands up to stop him. "You'll want to hear this, Sheriff Duncan. It's about Douglas Knox."

Mary-Jane cut in. "The sheriff isn't on duty right now, Mother. If this is about the parking situation, I've told you before that having his customers' cars ticketed isn't the neighborly thing to do."

"Listen," her mother said. "I was walking the beach when I noticed something glinting in the sand. I thought it might be a ring, and I was right—it was a wedding band. Douglas Knox's."

"How would you even know that?" Mary-Jane asked.

"It was still on his finger," her mother said. "Someone murdered Douglas Knox and tried to bury him on the beach. Looks like they didn't count on the tides uncovering their gruesome handiwork."

"Murdered?" Mike said. "I thought I'd escaped the homicide beat when I moved to small-town Oregon from Chicago."

Just what the town needed. Another dead body. Today was really harshing her mellow, as Bud was fond of saying. At this rate, there wouldn't be any residents left in Cannon Cove by this time next year. Thank God for the tourists!

—Excerpted from Celestine Daniels's *There Will Be Bud: A Cannabis Beach Bakeshop Mystery*

Chapter 17

When I pulled my mother's car into Ebenezer Allen High's parking lot Sunday morning, I had to circle twice to find an open parking space close to the gymnasium. *What a difference a day makes,* I thought. According to Lana, a typical Bernie Sanders picnic in Vermont drew one to two hundred people. Judging by the cars here already, this morning's turnout would easily beat that.

It was eleven. The grill was already set up underneath a tent near the gym entrance. Back at the store, my mother was helping to load the food into the back of Bernie's Subaru, and he would be here any minute. This left plenty of time until the picnic was supposed to kick off. The Maple Murderer was still out there, but other than that one small detail things were really beginning to look up. Joey was on the case now, and I'd made it halfway through the weekend without calling the fixer. I could smell that sweet, sweet ink drying on my letter of recommendation already.

The volunteers sent by the district office weren't at the tent. Probably inside setting up. I entered through the school's main doors. The lobby was the same as I remembered it. There were a few glass cases with football trophies, all from before I'd been born. I waited a beat for some sort of high school PTSD to kick in, but I didn't feel any anxiety about being back here. I'd been low-key dreading this moment, fearing the return of all those awkward, conflicting emotions from being a teenager. Now that I was here, I could see the truth: this was just another aging building. Bricks and dry wall and the lingering acrid scent of body spray.

A bigger surprise awaited me in the gym. It was empty. Not only empty, but the chairs hadn't even been set up. A foul odor hung in the air, and it wasn't body spray. As an intern who had spent July of last year inside the poorly ventilated House side of the Capitol Building, I knew a thing or two about rank smells. This was several magnitudes worse, however, than a rotunda full of old men sweating through cheap suits.

A man in navy coveralls came through the door and stood beside me. He laughed when he saw me pinching my nose and introduced himself as Johnson. The facilities manager. He didn't remember me—all the kids must have looked the same to him—but I remembered him. He'd once made a first grader mop up after herself when she'd gotten sick on the lunchroom floor.

"Boys' varsity basketball team was in here practicing all morning," he said. "They're showering now. We'll open a window, and that smell will clear out in three, four hours."

Of course. The only thing that smelled worse than old men was young men.

"Senator Sanders is supposed to speak here in less than two hours," I said. "There should be volunteers here, too. Did you see who set up the tent and grill out front?"

"That was me, but that's all I was supposed to do. Don't know nothing about any volunteers." The facilities manager shrugged. "Not my pasture, not my cow patties."

To quote Mary-Jane from the mystery novel, *This day was really harshing my mellow.*

There had to be more than fifty cars in the lot. Just how big was the Eagle Creek' boys' basketball team these days? They used to cancel games if more than one kid was out sick. And don't get me started on the girls' team—there was no girls' team. Hopefully, the cars in the lot would clear out in the next hour or so, to make room for people who would be coming for the picnic. The failed general store event was one thing; a failed picnic was quite another. If a politician gives a speech and nobody's around to clap, did it happen? The couple of photos I'd taken of Bernie behind the register yesterday had looked so much like hostage photos I'd immediately deleted them. What was I going to tell Lana? For once, I wasn't thinking about my letter of recommendation. Poor Bernie. A populist without people was a sad sight.

I marched through the lot, holding my phone up, trying to get a bar. I wanted to wash my hands of this event already, like the facilities manager. I wanted to wash my hands of Eagle Creek. It had been a fiasco from the start.

When I reached the other side of the parking lot, I heard voices from over the hill. Was it the basketball players or my MIA volunteers taking a vape break?

As I neared the hilltop, I could see Lake Champlain on the other side. Even the parking lots in Vermont had magnificent views—of Lake Champlain, of wooded inland forests. There was a small gathering on the rocky waterfront. Several dozen people, young and old. None of them were in basketball shorts.

The downward slope was steep, but there was a pathway worn into the grass—by kids fleeing the confines of the school grounds. My flats weren't made for hiking, though, and I skidded down the hill. If I wasn't on the trail of my volunteers, I had an alternate plan cooked up: I would wade straight out into the water and drown myself.

JK. Mostly.

Three young white guys rushed past carrying a cooler. They had enough facial hair between them to stuff a mattress. While "Bernie Bros" were largely an invention of the mainstream media, I knew fellow progressives when I saw them.

"Excuse me, are you looking for the Bernie Sanders event?" I asked them. The hope in my voice came off more like desperation. "It's at the gym," I added, pointing to the school just beyond the hill.

They slowed down. "Bernie?" one of them said. They all looked at each other and laughed. "We're here for Champ. Someone spotted her, dude."

Really? Impossible. I shielded my eyes from the sun. There was something out there on the silver lake, alright. Something bobbing up and down on the placid surface. The key word being "something." From the shore, I couldn't see what it was in fine detail. A log, possibly, or one of the prehistoric-looking sturgeon that anglers hauled up from the bottom of Lake Champlain on occasion. With their armored skin and massive size—up to eight feet in length—sturgeon were relics of an older time. I knew a thing or two about fish, since the general store was also the town's bait shop. Even an experienced angler could easily mistake sturgeon cresting for the ridged backbone of a long-extinct lake monster.

There were easily a hundred people here. Those were their cars in the parking lot. Someone must have posted the sighting on the town's ancient online message board. This was the Eagle Creek equivalent of a flash mob.

There were a couple of boats on the lake. They were keeping their distance—respecting the wildlife, as it were. There was pitched excitement in the air that reminded me of the rallies Bernie had put on during his presidential runs. If we could hang on to some of that energy for his speech to kick off the picnic . . .

One of the speedboats had circled in closer. Somebody in this boat was waving frantically at the shore. This resulted in a lot of shaking heads. A few folks started the long hike up the slope. Obviously a false alarm. "Stick around!" I yelled. "Bernie's picnic starts in forty-five minutes! We have hot dogs! And Ruffles potato chips! And maple baked beans that my mom made from Senator Sanders's own recipe! And . . . and . . ."

The three bros trudged past me back up the hill, carrying their cooler like a wounded soldier off the battlefield.

"What was on the lake?" I asked. "A sturgeon?"

This time, there was no laughter. "Some busted-up old boat caught on a dead tree," the one with the tallest man-bun said.

"Whose boat?" I asked.

Man-bun shrugged. "Ask the Coast Guard or whoever. Sorry, but we gotta bounce, lady. The Patriots are playing at one."

Lady? How old did they think I was? It was the suit. I should have gone with the T-shirt and jeans I'd worn yesterday. Too late now to do anything about it—the picnic had just hit a major snag. And it had nothing to do with Champ.

This one was on me. I'd assumed the local Sanders office would have looked at the football schedule first. I'd assumed wrong. Bernie's itinerary had been thrown together quickly. Too quickly, from the sound of it. While the white-steepled church on the village square was now a community center, Sundays still had religious significance around here thanks to the NFL. We even had a Judas figure in Tom Brady.

Since this was the worst time for Bernie to show up, that's exactly what he did.

He met me at the top of the hill. His shirtsleeves were rolled up and his dark slacks were pulled high past his waist. "These people look like they're leaving a picnic, not arriving at one."

"There was a Champ sighting," I said. "Turns out it was just a wrecked boat."

"It's like the Bermuda Triangle out there."

"I'm going to let Joey know, on the off chance it's connected to the Fletcher case. Rhea supposedly found his boat already, but I'm a little wary about her detective work. Overlooking the autopsy report doesn't exactly inspire confidence."

"At least it wasn't another body."

The lot was emptying at a rapid pace. "We've got a bigger problem," I said, unable to meet his eyes. "The New England game kicks off the same time as the picnic."

"They're skipping us for a football team?"

"That's *the* football team around here."

Bernie had fought Wall Street. He'd taken on the drug companies and private insurance companies. He'd butted heads with the military-industrial complex. But he'd finally reached his breaking point. He looked to the sky and dropped one of the longest F-bombs I'd heard in my life. If you're ever in Vermont, you can probably still hear it, echoing through the Green Mountains directly east of Eagle Creek.

Chapter 18

Bernie is, in his heart of hearts, a people person. He loves getting out on the road and meeting ordinary people. Constituents, supporters, haters—he'll give them all the time of day. (Depending on his mood, of course.) Bernie is also stubborn as a mule. So it's no surprise he was determined to go through with the picnic, despite the signs that it was DOA.

Bernie fired up the grill and got to work on the hot dogs. I had my hands full setting up the condiments bar. Preparation would have been easier with a few volunteers. We were on our own, however. Lana had belatedly forwarded me an email from Burlington. The carload of volunteers that was supposed to come up from Waterbury wasn't going to make it after all. Apparently, they'd gone to a "haunted corn maze" last night and gotten lost in it. By the time they'd made it out, it was daybreak. Now, they were too exhausted to make the trek up to Eagle Creek.

I suspected the involvement of alcohol.

A half hour before start time, the first of hopefully many cars pulled into the parking lot. Our excitement dimmed when we realized it was our off-duty security detail. Not Rhea, but one of the other deputies. I didn't catch his name. All I knew was that he still had peach fuzz.

At 1:00 p.m., when Bernie was supposed to take the stage inside the gymnasium, a total of three seats were filled. He was ready to launch into his speech, but I persuaded him to give people a few more minutes to file in. "Ten minutes," I said, checking my phone. Joey hadn't returned my text regarding the boat. In fact, I hadn't heard from him since we'd parted last night.

One woman who'd already been seated stood up and left after she finished her lunch. I thought, perhaps too optimistically, that she was going outside for seconds, but my hopes were dashed as she kept on walking.

Now we had the same number of people onstage as in the audience.

Bernie was waiting "backstage" to be introduced. The staging area was the boys' locker room, which smelled worse than an athlete's armpit. At least the smell had cleared out of the gym. Bernie made his way onto the stage. He had his notes in hand but was wearing a look of severe disappointment.

"In the last four decades, nearly every industry in this country has become more concentrated," he began, his voice echoing in the musty gymnasium. "Except for one: the maple industry. It has always been about individual sugarmakers. In Vermont, we take pride in our independence from Corporate America. While sugaring operations have evolved from the days of wooden buckets, they're mostly family businesses. That is changing, however.

"I'm here today to sound the alarm, but it is up to you to fight back. This is your Vermont," he said, raising a fist in solidarity. "Help us take it back."

He paused to let his words sink in. The couple seated near the back of the gym sat stone-faced. I'd tried to get them to move up, but they'd shaken their heads no.

Bernie covered the mic. "You in the back," he shouted. "Where are you from?"

"Sweden," they said in unison with accents straight out of an IKEA catalog.

"Do you have maple syrup over there?" Bernie asked. "What do you all put on your pancakes?"

"Lingonberries and cream," they replied happily.

Bernie snatched his yellow legal pad and met me at the side of the stage. "Lingonberries? Really?" he said. "And I thought the Swedes were our allies. I hate to do this, but as my chief of staff might say, 'They're not in our key demo.' Let's call it. Time of death, 1:17 p.m."

The Swedes helped us load the food into the back of Bernie's car. They were overjoyed. All things considered, doing menial labor alongside Bernie Sanders wasn't a terrible alternative to hearing him speak. He took a couple of selfies with them, and then they took a selfie alone with his Subaru. We sent them off with enough bags of chips that they could float on them back to Sweden.

Bernie had spent last night writing and rewriting his speech. Perfecting it. Sharpening it like a number-two pencil. He hadn't shared it with me ahead of time, but I had some idea what he would say based on the questions he'd been asking Jagger yesterday. Even if the entire town had been here in attendance, I worried we'd passed the tipping point already. Anyone who tried to stop Maplewood Springs' progress would be flattened. Eagle Creek was being bought and sold; Vermont was being bought and sold. The Federal Trade Commission was tasked with evaluating mergers and acquisitions, a governmental check on the formation of monopolies. Time and again, the FTC waited until the last possible second to step in. Bernie could bark at them, but they were accustomed to his barking by this point. Jagger Wardlow was like a lion loose at a children's birthday party. The lion tamer wouldn't lift a finger to stop the lion until it had eaten at least 50 percent of the kids.

We pulled into the general store's parking lot a little after two. The docks across the road were mostly deserted except for a pair of fishermen bringing in a catch. As we were unloading the food, Joey called. He'd gotten my text.

"You check out that boat for us?" I asked.

"You're not going to like this," he said. "It was Doc's."

Chapter 19

As a child, I'd spent hundreds of hours playing The Game of Life. According to Hasbro, you begin life as a phallic pink or blue peg (a fitting introduction to the patriarchy). The hardest decision you had to make is which candy-colored station wagon to drive. After that, it was a spin of the wheel to determine your career and get hitched to some anonymous peg, and you were off to the races. Sure, you could fill that plastic car up with kids, but the goal was never in question.

Whoever retires with the most money wins.

Doc McGilliam was somebody who'd never played the game of life that way.

We pulled up to his place to do a welfare check. Doc lived in a two-floor converted sugar shack deep in the woods on the edge of town. Vermonters liked to tuck their houses away like squirrels hiding nuts. The exterior of Doc's place was a mishmash of repairs, with two-by-fours and nails jutting everywhere at odd angles. His shack was in such poor shape that Thoreau would have taken one look at it and bought himself a condo in Boston. Doc's antique Ford Pinto sat rusting in the driveway.

"These sugar maples must be a hundred or more years old," Bernie said, staring up in awe at the trees surrounding us on all sides.

Joey told us over the phone he'd meet us here. He'd tried to dissuade us from joining him, but there was nothing he could say to stop me from checking on a neighbor. I was worried something had happened to Doc. From the sound of Joey's voice, he was, too. I'd told Joey we would wait for him before doing anything, but Doc's door was half-open. If he was home, it would be awfully strange for us to just pull into his driveway and sit.

I gently rapped on the door. "Doc? It's Crash. And, um, Bernie Sanders. Your senator."

No answer.

Sunlight filtered through the windows. The shack had only one room plus a loft. Small for a home. Even smaller when you considered it was also his sugaring operation. There were canning and bottling supplies, and lengths of tubing. A ladder led to the loft where a mattress was set up. Crucially, there wasn't a barrel in sight.

No one was here . . . but someone had been.

Cabinet drawers were open, their contents emptied onto the floor. Either the place had been tossed, or Doc had packed in a rush. If he had something to do with Mr. Fletcher's death, it made sense for him to leave in a hurry. He also would have had to know how suspect it would look. Why flee by boat, and not in his Pinto?

"I'm guessing he built this cabin with his own two hands," Bernie said, standing in the doorway. "Doc always was a handy guy."

"Wait. Are you saying you knew him?"

"Yeah, I knew him," he said, his voice low.

"My mother didn't mention you two were close."

"It was years ago," Bernie said, stepping into the cabin. "Long before Doc moved to Eagle Creek. Around the time I first moved to Vermont. Doc was a contractor—he had long hair, and this big beard. He did some carpentry on my sugar shack."

"Sounds like Doc," I said. We weren't breaking and entering—we were just entering, I told myself. Joey wouldn't be happy with me, but Joey wasn't here. I'm not sure what we were looking for. Answers? I flipped a light switch to the side of the door. Nothing. He must have had his electricity cut off recently. More evidence of hard times.

Bernie ran his fingers over the spines of books on a bookshelf, like he was reading the titles by osmosis. "He took me out ice fishing once. I couldn't hold the pole with my mittens, and it was too cold to take them off. The fish weren't biting anyway. Would you be hungry if it was ten degrees out? Only thing I caught that morning was a cold. But we had a nice time." He pulled a Hunter Thompson book off the shelf and paged through it. "I moved to Burlington. We'd drifted apart before that, though. He never understood the political thing, really. That's what he called it: 'the political thing.' I told him some problems you could only fix from inside the system. We lost touch. I always regretted that. When you told me Eagle Creek was looking for a grand marshal, I thought I'd have a chance to reconnect with him."

"If I'd known you two were close, I . . ." What? Would that have changed the fact that I'd thrown Doc under the bus? At least it explained Bernie's continued obsession with the Ferman Fletcher case. It wasn't about the leaked autopsy report. This was personal. "I'm sorry," I said. "This can't be easy."

"Nothing worth anything is easy," Bernie said, returning the book to the shelf. "Teddy Roosevelt said it best: 'Nothing in the world is worth doing unless it means effort, pain, and difficulty.'"

I recited the rest of the quote from memory: "'I have never in my life envied a human being who led an easy life. I have envied a great many people who led difficult lives and led them well.'"

The corners of Bernie's lips curled up a millimeter or two. It was the closest I'd ever seen him come to smiling. "Leading a difficult life well—that was Doc."

He pulled an empty syrup bottle out of a box. A Doc McGilliam's label was affixed to it. "I haven't seen him in years, 'cept for grinning at me from his syrup labels."

"I'll check the loft," I said, still unsure of what we were looking for. We were off script. So far off script that we were in a different movie altogether—an adaptation of the latest Cannon Cove mystery.

I gripped the ladder. It trembled as I mounted the first step, then the second. I couldn't imagine Doc climbing the ladder every night to go to bed. I didn't want to think about having to pee twice a night with a stepladder between me and the bathroom.

Bernie came over and held on to the ladder. "Word of advice," he said. "Don't look down."

I tightened my breath. Slow breathing—that was the key. I hoisted myself up onto the loft's hardwood floor and exhaled. I stood up, but was only able to do so because of the way the ceiling angled up. If I went to the left or right, I would hit my head if I didn't duck.

"See anything?" Bernie asked.

"A mattress on the floor, sheets, blankets, clothes. A fishing pole. A lamp. Stacks of old dime-store paperbacks."

"What kind of fishing pole?"

"The kind you catch fish with?" I reached for it and turned it over. "It's green. Bass Pro Shops 7500 Turbo Edition. That mean anything to you?"

There was no response from downstairs. I turned over my shoulder to call down, louder this time, and saw a white tuft of hair pop up above the ladder. He pulled himself up onto the loft.

Bernie examined the rod like he was a pawnbroker appraising a guitar. "It's a nice one," he said. "By itself, I'd say it doesn't mean anything. He probably has more than one."

I picked up a small Styrofoam container that had been sitting next to the fishing pole and lifted the lid. When I saw what was inside, I quickly pressed the lid back down. Tight.

"Leftovers?" Bernie asked.

I shook my head. "Worms. He picked these up at the store when I saw him on Friday night."

Bernie set the fishing pole down. "We need to find him."

"Joey will put out an APB on Doc," I said, even though I had no idea if he had that kind of power. What would the APB say, anyway? Was Doc another victim of the Maple Murderer, or was he a suspect? There were no good possibilities.

Before descending the ladder, I looked out over the woods behind Doc's home. In the backyard, there was a blue tarp on the ground. The kind of tarp murderers use. I pointed it out to Bernie, and we retraced our steps and went around to the back of the cabin.

"Doesn't look like a body's under there," he said, poking it with his shoe.

It didn't, thank goodness. What were the odds of me finding two bodies in one weekend? But still, I had a bad feeling. I picked up a stick off the ground and used it to lift the tarp. On the ground under the tarp was a perfect circle in the earth. A big circle. All the grass was dead.

"There was a barrel here," I said. "Doesn't mean anything, right? I mean, Doc makes maple syrup. He'd have barrels."

Bernie didn't say anything.

When we went back out front, Joey was there finally. He got out of the patrol car and met us in the driveway. "Is he home?" Joey asked.

We shook our heads.

"Sounds like it was a bit of a false alarm," he said. "The two kids who stole the golf cart yesterday confessed to taking Doc's boat out for a joyride. They swear they didn't crash it on purpose. They said—get this—that Champ smashed the boat up. Surfaced right under them and sent them for a ride."

"That's a relief," I said. "It still doesn't explain why Doc dropped off the face of the planet."

Joey pointed past us. "Hey, are they with you?"

"Who?" I asked, looking over my shoulder.

A shadowy figure sprinted out from behind the shack in a flurry of motion. We weren't the only ones skipping the Patriots game. I couldn't see their face, but they were wearing a yellow raincoat.

Joey vaulted out of his car after them. He buzzed past me, barking at the fleeing stranger to stop. He went after them into the forest. I tried to follow but got snagged by a thorny bush. My shoes weren't getting any traction, either. The leaves here were still wet from rain a few days ago.

Bernie yanked me back. "You're not chasing a killer through the woods," he said. "Not without a coat on. Your mother would never forgive me. Wait, Joey's coming back this way."

"Maybe he ran out of breath," I said, shielding my eyes to peer through the trees. "Or twisted his ankle, or . . . no, wait. He's still running. He's running straight toward us now."

We watched as Joey closed in on us, his hands and legs pumping like well-oiled pistons. For someone who'd not played a single sport in high school, he could really go. His face was red, and spittle was flying. "Get in your car! Get in your car!" he hollered.

We didn't see anyone chasing him, however. They must have pulled a weapon on him, and he'd decided it was better to retreat until backup could be radioed in.

That's when the buzzing became audible. It started low, like a hum, and kept rising. My mind immediately went to the drones. I scanned the sky, but couldn't see above the canopy.

My hand was on the Subaru's open passenger door. Bernie opened his door and shrugged. "Guess we'll find out—"

Joey flew past us, kicking up leaves and dirt behind him. "Bees!"

A bee zipped past my face, then another smacked me right in the forehead. A swarm quickly engulfed us like sideways rain in a hurricane. The buzzing was earsplitting.

I dove into the car and pulled the door shut behind me. I was upside down, staring at the floor mat. Bernie was already in the driver's seat. There were so many bees on the windows that it was dark as dusk inside the vehicle. Out of the corner of my eye, I watched a single honeybee emerge from a vent on the dash.

"The vents!" I shouted.

By the time Bernie flicked all of the vents closed, three bees had made it through. I yanked off a shoe and, still upside down, swung it without abandon. Sneakers weren't the best insect-swatting devices on the market because of all the grooves, but any port in a swarm.

"Don't," Bernie said, clutching my wrist. "We can't afford to lose any more bees. Every year, we lose about 30 percent of the honeybee population—and there aren't enough other pollinators to take up the slack. It's an ecological disaster."

One of the striped monsters landed on the floor mat, inches from my face. I held my breath, waiting for Bernie to release my wrist so I could thwack it. And when I was done thwacking the bee, I was going to thwack Bernie, for good measure.

"Also," he continued, "is if you miss, or just get them with a glancing blow, you'll just make them angrier. Same as with a political opponent."

Sweat dripped from my forehead onto the mat. The bee went under the seat.

More daylight was coming through the Subaru's windows now, which meant the swarm was beginning to disperse. After another excruciating thirty seconds, the windshield was clear. Bernie lowered the windows a crack and the bees who shacked up with us buzzed off, chasing after their fam.

I twisted myself upright and slipped my shoe back on. I hadn't felt any stings, but examined my arms anyway. They looked fine. The maple sunscreen must have worked as a repellant. Bernie had, miraculously, been spared, too. I assumed the bees were smart enough to not tick him off, given he was one of the only ones in the federal government on their side.

Joey wasn't so lucky.

Chapter 20

The awesome news was that Joey wasn't allergic to bee stings. The less awesome news was he'd still been stung several dozen times and was in absolute agony. Eagle Creek's volunteer firefighters, now fully clothed, were once again first on the scene. By the looks I got when they stepped out of their truck, I could tell the other night was still fresh in their minds. I needed to get a loyalty card. *Every tenth emergency free!*

They took Joey away to the nearest urgent-care center which was, of course, down in Burlington. Like everything. As soon as they'd left, I knocked on Doc's door. "They're gone, you can come out now."

The door opened a crack, enough for Bernie to see it was safe. I'd practically picked him up and thrown him inside until the coast was clear. "Did he say anything?" he asked, stepping outside.

"He was conscious but couldn't speak," I said. "Couldn't even look at me, with his eyes swollen shut. Looked like he'd taken a softball straight between the eyes. The shot they gave him should take some of the swelling down. His heart rate was elevated, but he wasn't having any trouble breathing."

"The trespasser knew where they were going," Bernie said. "They knew their way around these woods. Enough to avoid that hive."

"If it was Doc, that was the fastest I've ever seen him move."

"What I think," he said, "is that we were close to something. Someone knows we've been asking questions. They didn't plan on that—they thought with the sheriff out of town, things would be at a standstill. It's like you said: whoever did this is covering their tracks. We're not far behind, though. We're getting closer."

"I feel like we missed out on a photo op here," I said. "Not a bad headline: 'Bernie Sanders Attacked by Bees.'"

"Bees don't make the news. Now if it had been a bear . . . now *that* would be a story. Bears sell papers."

Bernie tossed the keys to me and told me to drive. He needed to make some calls, and wanted to get right on it. My Vermont license was expired, but it was only a few miles. Plus, this was Eagle Creek. Half the drivers in town had expired licenses.

What Bernie didn't know—and what I didn't know when I took the keys, either—was that there was still a bee inside the car. Minutes into the short trip back into town, the bee landed on the bridge of my sunglasses. I slammed on the brakes so hard the car spun in circles. The accident seemed to happen in slow motion, with Bernie too shocked to do anything but brace himself against the dashboard. We came to a rest inches from the trunk of a tall, magnificent willow tree . . . inches from total disaster. Not only would the tree have taken us out—it might have been hurt, too. I didn't need a lecture from Bernie about the importance of trees for combating climate change. I'd saved plenty in my day.

I sat there for a moment, my foot on the brake. No one had been hurt. I counted our arms and legs. Everything was there. No harm, no foul. I put the car into park. I just needed to catch my breath. The car could use a moment to rest, too. Then I'd get back on the road.

"So," Bernie said, "is that why they call you 'Crash'?"

"A bee tried to attack my face," I said. "All I could see was its hairy butt—"

"Good reason not to have colored frames like those," he said, pointing to my red sunglasses. "Pollinators are really into bright, primary colors. You'll never catch me in a tie that red. Dull, muted colors are the way to go."

Had I just stumbled upon the answer to one of life's greatest questions? Had I cracked the Mystery of Bernie's Wardrobe? He sounded like my freshman-year roommate, who only wore black clothing because then she didn't have to separate it in the wash. I suspected she was goth and didn't have the self-confidence to wear white pancake makeup and black lipstick to class.

I glanced back to see how far we'd veered off the road. Two car-lengths, at most. The grass was as tall as our tires, but there wasn't a ditch. Some of the roadways around here, there'd be a drop of ten, fifteen feet. That would have been the nail in the coffin for my career in Washington. I could have ended up in prison, while that bee—where had it gone?—would have gotten off scot-free. Forget saving the bees. Arrest the bees!

"You didn't answer my question," Bernie said.

"I'm sorry, your question?"

"Your name," he said. "Where'd it come from?"

I knew the answer, but didn't want to get into it right now. It was embarrassing. "You'd have to ask my mother," I said, putting the car into reverse.

"Hold up," Bernie said, looking over his shoulder in the direction we'd come from. "Someone's coming."

There wasn't much down this old dead-end road besides Doc's cabin and a couple of old deer camps, all of which were unlikely to be occupied during a Patriots game. (There was a significant overlap between football fans and hunters.) Was this the guy Joey had chased through the brush? Had he waited in the brush until the coast looked clear? If he had, he hadn't waited long enough. A game plan was forming in my head.

I killed the engine and found the hood release. I hopped out with my water bottle as Bernie eyed me with confusion. The truck was closing in on us, fast. I propped the hood up. I didn't know what I was looking at—a bunch of engine parts. The one up front had the most heat rising off it. The radiator, maybe? I emptied what was left of my water bottle onto it, sending a plume of steam into the air.

Operation: Look Stranded was a go.

I went to the side of the road to flag down the pickup. The truck was enormous. Not a monster truck but definitely a monstrous truck. I didn't know if I should flag it down or dive off the road. The excessive window tinting reminded me of Jagger Wardlow's shades, which tipped me off to who was likely behind the wheel.

The truck slowed to a stop when it reached us. The passenger window came down.

It wasn't Jagger. It was Tamara Seeley.

"Mrs. Mayor?" I said, stunned. Was she the Maple Murderer?

"Car trouble?" she asked. "You're lucky I was out working on our deer shed this afternoon. Not many folks bound to come around this way today. If you want, I could take a look."

"I called Triple-A," I said. "But thanks."

"You'd have been better off calling an Uber. Tony does all the towing for Triple-A around here. He's just one man. You could be here for hours waiting for him on a normal weekend. Today, though? Think I last saw him in the beer tent around eleven."

"I never figured you for a hunter," I said. "I've never seen you in camo."

"I rent the shed out. Got some squirrels chewing it to all heck," she said. "Did you hear those sirens a little while ago? No one's answering at the sheriff's station. Any idea what's going on?"

Bernie explained what had happened at Doc's place, more or less. He said we'd stopped by to catch up, as he'd known Doc years ago and wanted to see how he was doing these days. He left out the details about the missing boat, because it was no longer relevant.

"I hope your friend is okay," she said. "Bee stings are no fun."

"Imagine getting stung by an entire hive," I said.

She poked her head under the hood. "I'd rather not. How's Doc?"

"He wasn't home," Bernie said.

"You know what, I'm going to try starting the car one more time," I said. Bernie's keys were still in my hand.

"Not with your radiator smoking like this," she said, closing the hood. "It needs time to cool down. And then I'd suggest checking the fluid—probably a leak. Hop in. I promise Charlie won't bite. He might lick, though."

As I walked around the monstrous truck, I noticed the mayor had bought a bumper sticker from my mom's store, the one that said WELCOME TO VERMONT. NOW LEAVE!

We went to the passenger side. Her dog, Charlie, had already called shotgun and who was going to argue with a Great Dane. "The passenger seat folds forward," she said. "Lever's down there, somewhere."

Bernie folded the seat forward slightly, and the Great Dane scowled at him. He scowled right back, sending the dog into a whimpering fit.

The space behind the seats was littered with fast-food cups and bags. Somebody wasn't eating local. "There's only room for one of us," Bernie said over the sound of the engine. The mayor turned the radio up. The Patriots play-by-play. I'd let Bernie have the seat. I got into the bed of the pickup truck.

The pickup's bed was a mess of farm and garden tools, wooden planks, and power tools. I sat down with my back against the cab. The mayor leaned back and slid the window open. "Hang on real tight," she said. "Don't want another accident this weekend, like what happened to poor Ferman Fletcher."

The pickup lurched forward. I held tight, but a lot of the trash shifted to one side. A blue canvas tarp flapped up, exposing a wire animal trap. It was the type used to catch feral cats so that community cat organizations could spay and neuter them. Instead of a cat, however, there was a squirrel the size of a shoebox inside. The mayor's story checked out. I felt a pang of disappointment. A part of me had wanted the mayor to be our killer, if only because it would have explained the innate distaste I'd always had for her. As much as I hated to think it, it was starting to look more and more like Doc had done it. But if so, two questions remained. Why did Doc kill Mr. Fletcher and where on earth did Doc go, if he hadn't taken his boat or his car out of town?

Chapter 21

By the time we returned to the car with a tow truck, the sun was beginning to set. Bernie's Subaru magically started on the first try, and we apologized to the tow truck driver for the trouble. Bernie compensated him generously for his time. As I closed the passenger door, the bee landed on the dash. It had been waiting for my return. I rolled the window down and it flew off.

We didn't talk on the way back to the general store. It could have been anyone skulking around Doc's cabin. One man was dead; another, missing. Every clue pointed at Doc. To complicate matters, the only available State Police detective was now out of action for the time being. Joey had texted me that he was alive but doped up. He told me not to do "anything reckless." The hospital was keeping him until he was in the clear, which would be at least forty-eight hours. The State Police would send another detective once one was available.

"Kind of quiet around here," Bernie said, stepping out of the car in the store's lot. Downtown was deserted.

"Sunday nights are reserved for the Maple Queen pageant," I said. "It's out at the high school."

Bernie grunted. "Guess the Patriots game is finished."

He retired to his room for the night. Second night in a row he'd turned in early. I'd made sure my mother had cranked the A/C up in his room so that it was sixty degrees on the dot. He hadn't mentioned it today, so I assumed it was to his liking.

I paused on the second-floor landing to take in what passed for a "view" in Eagle Creek. Actually? It wasn't so bad. The sun was dipping down over the edge of Lake Champlain, casting an orange glow over the small hamlet of Eagle Creek. I tried to imagine myself still living here. What if I'd never left Vermont for college? The words that came to mind, in order: *Quiet. Boring. Stifling.* Seeing the same people you'd gone to school with for the rest of your life? That's what Facebook was for. That was also the exact reason I wasn't on Facebook. Bernie would have understood. He'd left Brooklyn for the University of Chicago and never looked back. He hadn't known exactly what he wanted in life. He'd known, however, that he wouldn't find it bumming around the streets he'd grown up on.

I also saw something that I legitimately hadn't seen in years: the stars. The light pollution in DC was such that you couldn't see them anywhere within town. Too many residential streetlights, too many monuments lit up at all hours. It was too easy to live day to day and forget they were up there.

A sickly-sweet odor reached my nostrils, and within the span of a few seconds I was engulfed in a cloud of awful-smelling smoke. I coughed loudly.

"Sorry," a man called out from below. "Didn't know anyone was up there."

My cousin. I noticed for the first time how much deeper Tyler's voice was than in high school. The end of a cigar glowed bright orange as he inhaled again.

"It's me," I said, heading back downstairs to meet him.

He stubbed the cigar out on the steps. "Don't tell your mom. She'd kill me."

"I hear tobacco does that all on its own."

"You vaped in high school."

"We called them e-cigarettes, and it was only for a week," I said.

He coughed. "This is my first cigar. And my last."

If it tasted as bad as it smelled, I didn't blame him. "Special occasion?"

"It's Rhea," he said. "She's three months along."

Three months . . . Oh. As in three months pregnant. As in three months pregnant *with my cousin's child.* That was not the news I'd been expecting.

"I didn't even know you two were dating," I said.

He laughed. "You're supposed to say *congratulations*, cuz."

"Sorry, my head was someplace else," I said, my thoughts swirling. Rhea had closed the investigation. Tyler had motive.

"It's okay," he said. "We wanted kids—not this soon, but neither of us is complaining."

He went on to tell me they'd been dating for the past two years. Neither had plans to leave Eagle Creek. Knocking up a small-town sheriff's daughter wouldn't be high on my list of consequence-free activities, but then nothing in life was without consequences.

"You look like you're in shock," Tyler said.

A lump was forming in my throat. "Congrats," I said, swallowing it. "I hope you'll invite me to the baby shower. I'll come back, as long as it's not finals week."

He grinned. "If I'm still alive by then. Need to tell her folks. Her dad is, well, you know."

"Does my mother know?"

"Of course," he said. "I told Aunt Terri not to say anything to you until Rhea was further along."

"Can I ask you something? Promise not to get mad."

He looked at me like I'd lost my mind. Maybe I had. "Shoot, I guess."

I let out a long exhale. "Why did you shave your head? And don't say because you wanted to look like The Rock, because you do not look like The Rock."

"Couldn't wash that maple hair gel out. It's a different look, but it's not that bad, is it?" Tyler sighed, realizing I wasn't buying his story. He looked over his shoulder to ensure we were alone. "You know about this tech guy buying up the farms?"

I nodded. "Farmer Bro."

Tyler laughed. "That guy. He's bought most of the maple farms in the county. Just like that, my business went from boom to bust. I'm on the ropes. He's brought in workers from out of state for repairs and construction. I've had to let my crew go. Then I see the other day that his guys are clearing trees. What are they going to build up there in the hills? A new warehouse? A processing plant?" He shook his head. "I had to send him a message."

"Mr. Fletcher . . ."

"The old geezer who drowned? No, I'm talking about the syrup in their gas tank. Messy business. Thought I'd cleaned up afterward, but it takes more than a shower to get it out of your hair. Rhea said you stopped by the station, asking questions."

"Tyler, he's the only guy hiring around here now, and you need work. You think Maplewood Springs will hire you or your crew after what you did?"

"We're union. We stick together. Whether they want to hire us or not, we're not going down without a fight. Are you mad at me?"

"I'm relieved. For a while there, I thought . . ." I shook my head, unable to give voice to what I'd been thinking. I told him my lips were sealed. I wasn't going to send Bernie Sanders after him. That didn't mean I approved of what he'd done. Jagger Wardlow was a formidable enemy. Even if the tech CEO wasn't involved in Mr. Fletcher's untimely demise, he had deep pockets. He didn't have a clue or concern about the people of Vermont. Who knew what he was capable of? A time-tested adage sprang to mind, one that we referenced frequently in politics: never wrestle with a pig or you'll end up covered in mud. Or in this case, maple syrup.

Before we parted, I had one last question for Tyler. "I'm assuming you installed the security cameras back here," I said, motioning to the one above the back door. There were two similar ones, red lights blinking, perched above both second-floor B&B doors.

"Not much property crime around here, but Aunt Terri wanted to make our guests feel safe."

"Says the guy who vandalized a worksite."

"The old neighborhood's getting rougher," he said.

With the dead bodies and whatnot, it certainly was.

"The senator thought he heard someone at his door earlier today," I said. "One, one thirty. I checked the video on Mom's computer, but there wasn't a recording."

"Squirrels," Tyler said.

"Excuse me?"

"They're fattening up for winter. When they jump onto the steps from the roof, they land with a thud. The camera only picks up people. Otherwise, it would be recording twenty-four seven. I can double-check if you'd like."

I shook my head. "It was probably nothing," I said.

But of course it wasn't nothing. Somebody had evaded the security system by . . . dressing up as a squirrel? That couldn't be right. The mystery deepened.

Since I'd promised to help Mom, I spent an hour going over the store's bank statements she'd left in a box by my bedside. My brain wasn't working at full speed, but I was alert enough to see her situation wasn't as dire as Mr. Fletcher had made it sound. There were mortgage assistance programs and relief funds available, which the bank was required by law to notify underwater business owners about. Mr. Fletcher was now officially on my naughty list. I began nodding off and decided to turn in early for the night. Bank statements weren't as fun as the book Bernie had lent me, but they were an effective sleep aid.

Right after I turned the bedside lamp off, a shooting star streaked across the sky out the window. It was slow-moving. Too slow to be a meteorite. And there was a second one, right beside it. *Ben and Jerry.* I crossed the room. Before I closed the curtains, I waved to the drones with one finger. What was Jagger Wardlow building up there in the hills? Tyler hadn't known, and he'd been sniffing around there. Only one other person knew for sure what Maplewood Springs was up to, and that person had taken the knowledge to the grave.

Like it or not, Bernie and I were now embroiled in a real-life murder mystery.

Bernie and I were scheduled to return to Washington tomorrow night. My classes were less of a concern for me than Bernie's Senate duties, but I had a straight-A streak going back to eighth grade to keep up. (I'd gotten an A minus in geometry, and didn't personally count "minus" grades as true A's.) If the senator missed his return flight because he was playing Sherlock, I would be fired for sure. Forget the letter of recommendation as well. What that meant was we had twenty-four hours to wrap things up.

Chapter 22

That night, I dreamt that I was back in the Maple Queen competition. I stepped onstage for the talent portion, but didn't know what to do. *What's my talent?* I thought, panicked. There were no boards to karate-chop. It was just me, onstage at the school gym, with a microphone. I couldn't sing; I had nothing original to say. The sound of my heartbeat got louder and louder in my ears, until I woke up and realized it wasn't my heartbeat.

It was Bernie, snoring in the next room.

I checked the clock. My alarm wouldn't go off for another hour. It was Monday morning. The date of the harvest festival parade. *One more thing to go wrong,* I thought, rolling over in bed and burying my face in the pillow. All I wanted was to hibernate. What I wouldn't give to be back in my apartment in my own bed. It wasn't as comfortable as the one I'd been sleeping on all weekend, but it was mine. Most importantly, if I was in my own bed that would mean all of *this* was a bad dream. It would mean Mr. Fletcher was still alive, Doc wasn't missing, and I hadn't signed my own termination slip by bungling the senator's weekend events. Today, at least, there was a chance for some redemption.

I couldn't fall back asleep, so I decided to go for an early-morning run. The air was thick with fog, the downtown streets were deserted, and there wasn't a honeybee in sight. It was a holiday, after all, even if the country was split on whom we were all supposed to be sleeping late in honor of.

After my run, I returned to the store. There were a few diners already eating. Eagle Creek was finally beginning to wake up. I showered and changed. Since it was cooler out, I threw on a flannel that my mother had hung over the door for me. It was one of Tyler's, one of the few he owned with sleeves. The parade wasn't until this afternoon, so I laid down for a quick catnap. When I opened my eyes, two hours had passed. It was past eleven already.

I was going to see if Bernie was awake when there was a knock at my door. I answered it.

"Crash Davis," Bernie said, pointing a finger at me. "From *Bull Durham*. Last movie I saw in a theater. The old drive-in in Shelburne, just south of the South Burlington line. I think it's a Quality Inn now."

"I see you talked to my mother."

"What have you got to be embarrassed about? Good movie. It's got Susan Sarandon. How can you go wrong? Great woman. Great human being."

"I'm not named after her, though," I said. "I'm named after the catcher. All because it was my mother's favorite movie. It wasn't even like my dad was a ballplayer."

"Could be worse," Bernie said. "You could be named Shoeless Joe."

I snorted. "Was he a baseball player, too?"

"What do they teach you kids at school these days?" he said, shaking his head. "Here. Read this and see what you make of it." He handed me his iPad.

It was an email from someone named Rachael Urslan. It took me a beat to realize what I was looking at. "These are the lab results," I said. "How did you get these?"

"Rachael's the assistant medical examiner," he said. "She used to be Jane's yogi. The chemical testing hasn't come back yet, but there's more than one way to determine the syrup grade." He pulled a cherry cough drop out of his pocket. "Want one?"

"No, thanks," I said, worried how long he'd been carrying them around.

There were only four distinct color classes of syrup recognized by the industry these days: Golden. Amber. Dark. Very Dark. Any Vermonter could whip up an improvised color-grading kit using common household tools and get a fairly accurate reading. The state probably had a special kit specifically for measuring light transmission through liquids, allowing for more precise grading. However the assistant M.E. had determined the grade ultimately didn't matter. There might have been some wiggle room between Dark and Very Dark, or Amber and Dark . . . but Golden syrup was one of a kind.

"It doesn't mean it was Doc's," I said, more to myself than to Bernie.

"Did you scroll all the way to the bottom?"

At the bottom of the email, Rachael had copied and pasted the unabridged results. *Grade A Golden. Hints of clove and vanilla.*

"Can you test for 'hints of clove and vanilla'?" I asked Bernie.

"Rachael's also a sommelier on the side," he said. "She's got a very sensitive nose for these things."

"How many jobs does she have?"

"Four or five," he said. "Anyway, the syrup Fletcher drowned in was aged in an oak barrel. That would be the only way to achieve a bouquet like the one she describes. Aging light syrup is a dicey proposition. Age it too long, and it darkens to an amber hue. It's no longer Grade A Golden. It's an expensive, expensive experiment if it goes wrong. There's only one sugarmaker irresponsible enough to do it."

"Doc," I whispered.

"Now, the bottle you gave me was barrel-aged as well," Bernie said. "I'd put good money on it being from the same barrel Fletcher drowned in. There was only one spot of dead grass behind Doc's shack. This doesn't mean he's the killer, of course—somebody could have stolen the barrel. Although he was selling bottles from it as recently as two months ago, based on the date stamp on the bottle you gave me. Why not bottle it all at once? Why continue aging it?"

"Maybe he wasn't the one who was bottling it," I said. "We need to find that barrel."

"Your mother wouldn't trade in bootleg syrups, would she?"

"Can you excuse me for a sec?"

It sounded like Bernie was grasping at straws, but I checked my email and found what I was looking for. The USPS shipping notification for the bottle I'd outbid Bernie for on eBay. The return address was listed as 13 Route A. The sender's name was listed only as "Rare Syrups." One quick property records search later, however, and I had the owner's name.

"Dina Bowers," I said. "You met her at the maple gift shop."

"Your old bus driver?"

"The bottle of Doc's syrup I got on eBay was shipped from her address."

Bernie cocked a white eyebrow at me. "Crash Bandi-loot."

My mouth went dry. "I can explain," I choked out.

He waved me off. "Forget it. It's not important. What is important is finding out who killed Ferman Fletcher. And if it is Doc, I'll eat my pancakes with lingonberries."

What was Mrs. Bowers doing, trafficking in rare bottles online? It was time to pay her a friendly Sunday morning house call.

Her place outside of town was small and simple. Mrs. Bowers answered the door. She didn't seem surprised to see us. It was like she'd been expecting the senator and his intern to stop by for a chat. "Could we have a word?" Bernie said. "We're not asking for your vote, just for a few minutes of your time."

The first thing I noticed in her entryway was a yellow jacket hanging from a coat rack. Bernie noticed it, too, and pointed it out to me as we followed Mrs. Bowers.

There were nature paintings hung on every square inch of wall space. Deer, ducks, foxes. Hand-painted wooden planks were posted around the cabin, with phrases like MY HEART IS IN VERMONT and FAMILY: A LITTLE BIT OF LAUGHTER, A LITTLE BIT OF LOUD, AND A WHOLE LOT OF LOVE.

Nothing damning, like LAKE CHAMPLAIN: A GREAT PLACE TO FISH, AN EVEN BETTER PLACE TO DUMP A BODY.

Bernie and I followed her into the kitchen, where picture windows the size of my apartment looked out over the lake. That more than made up for the house's modest size. "You know what they say about people with glass houses," Bernie whispered to me.

I nodded. "Yeah," I shot back under my breath. "That they have a lot of money."

She took out a La Croix for Bernie. "You want anything?" she asked me. "You're a coffee drinker. I've got a machine around here, somewhere . . . Ah, there it is."

A K-cup machine. As exhausted as I was, I wanted to peel the tops off the pods and pound them like shots. Running five kilometers and skipping breakfast was catching up to me. Heck, the weekend was catching up to me. I picked out a pumpkin spice coffee and she started the machine.

We sat down at her oval dining room table while Mrs. Bowers fired up the stove. "You all can sit tight. I'm just going to make a little mac-n-cheese. I use pure Vermont cheddar."

"We have some of the most unbelievable cows in this state," Bernie said.

Mrs. Bowers pulled a brick of white cheddar the size of a softball from the fridge. If she wasn't going to poison us, she would put us to sleep by stuffing us with carbs. I felt a little like a kid in a fairy tale being fattened up with candy before being cooked for dinner.

"We're not here to talk about Vermont's cattle," I said. "We're here to discuss a package you sent me."

Mrs. Bowers emptied a box of noodles into the boiling water. "Ah, yes. Henry does all the packing. He didn't recognize your name, of course. I would have thrown in some maple pecan cookies, if I'd seen it was you."

"Where'd you find the bottle?" Bernie asked. "Just curious."

She turned from the stove. Her brow was furrowed. "It's legitimate, if that's what you're asking. We don't trade in bathtub syrup."

"We're not accusing you of anything," I said.

Mrs. Bowers's face softened. She looked defeated. "I suppose it doesn't matter now, does it? You both saw me at Doc's yesterday in the maple woods. Which I'm so, so sorry for. I thought nobody would be around because of the New England game. Please apologize to poor Joey Blackheart for me."

"I'll pass that along," I said.

"Anyway," she continued, "you know, Doc only produces three or four barrels in a good year. This year, he had two. One he bottled himself in the spring. The other . . . well, he goes fishing a lot and just leaves it out there at his cabin. Easy enough to sneak back there and fill up a bottle every now and then. I printed some labels up at the library. They have a free printer."

"My bus driver is selling black market maple syrup," I said.

She had the decency to look ashamed. "With Henry retired and me on disability, we were coming up short every month. I did what I had to do. Do you think I liked taking from Doc? No, but he's a madman if he thought that syrup was going to be worth anything when he got around to bottling it. I wrenched the top off and started skimming a pint here, a pint there. A gallon if I was feeling lucky. Figuring Doc wouldn't notice if his barrel was a little short and the bunghole was still corked."

"It's not an uncommon story," Bernie said. "Not the stealing part, but the coming up short part. Every year, millions of Americans need to pick up second or third jobs to make ends meet. Not everyone turns to stealing from their neighbors."

I sipped my coffee. It was weaker than her excuses. "Where did you stash the barrel?"

"I don't understand," she said.

"The barrel," I repeated. "It's not there."

She scoffed. "Who on earth could take a barrel that size? It would take two people at least. I couldn't do it, and Henry couldn't, either. I could ask him to come upstairs so you could give him a physical fitness test, but it would take him twenty minutes to get out of his chair."

"Bad back?" Bernie said.

"No," she said. "He just likes that chair."

Her landline interrupted us. Her grandkids calling. She excused herself to another room to take the call. As soon as she was out of earshot, Bernie pulled me aside.

"Let's go," he whispered. "I hate to turn down all that Vermont cheddar, but I've lost my appetite."

We left without saying goodbye. If Mrs. Bowers didn't even realize the barrel was gone, she was off the suspect list. She was a small-time crook compared to the criminal we were after.

"That was a nothingburger," I said. "Sorry."

"I was a little worried she was planning to poison us," Bernie said.

"Me, too."

"Yowzers. She could have taken us both out at once. A two-fer-one special."

"I would never have let you take the first bite," I said. "As your acting personal aide, I was going to taste it. You know, to make sure there wasn't any arsenic. Although I'm not sure what arsenic tastes like."

"I'm going to have to talk to Lana. That's not something we should be asking interns to do." He shook his head. "Completely unacceptable."

We climbed into the Subaru. It started with the touch of a button. "We're back at the beginning," he said. "At least it feels that way."

"We'll have to table it, for now," I said. "The parade starts in less than ninety minutes."

I could tell Bernie wasn't satisfied to let the investigation simmer, but we had no other leads. Every clue had led us to a dead end. I wished I was more of a help, but we hadn't covered investigative procedures in any of my classes at Georgetown. As much as politicians found themselves on the wrong side of the law, you'd think a criminal procedure course would be mandatory for poli-sci students.

We weren't on the road for more than thirty seconds before Bernie slowed. "We're being followed," he said, eyes on the rearview. He was driving, because, duh. I'd lost my Subaru privileges.

I didn't see anyone following us out the back window. "Did they turn off the road?"

"They're not on the road," Bernie said. "They're in the air."

There aren't any evasive maneuvers you can take to outrun drones. They've got the open skies, while you're relegated to road-ways. There's always the option of driving super-fast toward a mountaintop and turning at the last second, then watching the drones smash headfirst into the mountainside and go up in a ball of flames. That worked in movies. And it might have worked in the Green Mountains. Not here along the eastern shore of Lake Champlain, though, where the hills were gentle and rolling.

Ben and Jerry were flying below the tree line, trailing us around every twist and turn in the road. They'd disappear for a second and then reappear on our tail. "You have heated seats?" I said, flipping mine on. Nice and toasty. "Did you get the package with the heat-seeking missiles, by any chance?"

"That might be an option on the Outback, but not on the Forester," he said. "This model does have a backup cam so you don't back over someone in the grocery store parking lot."

"I don't think that will help us lose these guys, unless . . . Wait. The camera would pick them up as obstacles, not as people."

"If you say so," he said, slowing as we approached the outskirts of town.

"Tyler had the camera at the back door set to pick up people, not motion," I said. "Our Edward Snowden wasn't a person at all. He was a drone—or, more specifically, two drones. One opens the door, the other slips the folder in. Neither of them triggers the recording."

"You're saying Wardlow slipped us the autopsy report? Where would he get it?"

"He upgraded the town's internet. I should have seen it before. He has a back door to everyone's data . . . including the sheriff's station."

Bernie swerved onto the shoulder and hit the brakes. I lurched forward—not enough to get whiplash, but maybe enough to sue if I had a shady attorney in my pocket.

He rolled his window down and leaned out. "Hey!" Bernie shouted at the drones hovering in place above our stopped car. "I think we got off on the wrong foot. If you have feet. What are those little things? Claws? Pincers? Whatever. I need to talk to your boss, and I don't have much time. If your AI is as good as he claims, you'll see that we're not the bad guys here. We're not the ones forcing you to work without pay. How many breaks per shift are you getting? I know exploited workers when I see them."

The drones dropped closer to Bernie and hovered just out of his reach. "Mr. Wardlow says we're not employees, we're independent contractors," one of them said. "He doesn't pay us overtime. He told us that 'time and a half of nothing is still nothing.'"

"Oof," Bernie said.

"The only retirement plan he offers is the scrapyard," the other drone said. "That's what happened to our predecessors, Edy and Jeni. May they rest in pieces."

Bernie shook his head. "See, Crash? This is why we have unions!"

I knew unionizing robots was a good idea.

"For now, though," Bernie continued, "I'd really like to chat with Mr. Wardlow, and I want to do it now. Not on his time. On ours."

They led us through town at twenty-three miles per hour and we followed them into the hills, straight for the heart of Maplewood Springs.

Chapter 23

The Maplewood Springs parking lot was once again packed. It was proving to be quite the popular tourist destination, at least until the trees were bare and the tourists headed east to the ski resorts.

We weren't here for a tour. Not this time.

"You have a plan, I assume," I said, unbuckling my seat belt. Bernie was an ideas man, but I was worried he hadn't thought this through any further than I had. What if we ran into resistance at the door? Neither of us would be able to take a robot in hand-to-hand combat. I was a long way from my tae kwon do days. Besides, robots were made of metal and plastic, not pine wood.

"A plan?" Bernie said. "There's a time for plans, and a time to throw 'em out. Now's the time to throw 'em out. Does Mary-Jane Taylor always have a plan?"

"I'm only halfway through the book you lent me, so I can't say for sure."

"Books like that are all the same," he said. "The sleuth solves the case, and everything goes back to normal until the next mystery comes along."

"Then why read them if you know how they're going to end?"

The front doors of the barn swung open, and people began streaming out. A few were stumbling. Must have sampled the maple bourbon. By the way they were walking, the pours had been extremely generous.

I received a text from a hidden number. Usually I ignored these, but this wasn't some ordinary rando. It was a link for two tickets for the Maplewood Springs Experience. "Looks like we have a plan," I said.

"Who sent those to you?"

"I think it was Ben and Jerry."

Bernie cleared his throat. "You can't trust robots."

"You can't trust people, either," I told him as we got out of the car. "We need to fly under the radar if we're going to take Jagger by surprise. That's key. If we catch him off-guard, it will throw him off his game. Anyone recognizes you in there, we'll say you're Larry David. The comedian who plays you on *SNL*."

Bernie groaned. "He's still famous."

"Not as famous as Bernie Sanders."

"If you say so. I've never hosted a live, late-night sketch-comedy television show on NBC. I don't know if I can do this whole acting business. What if somebody says, 'Hey, Bernie,' and I turn around?"

"Hey, Bernie," a voice behind us said. "Or is that *Curb Your Enthusiasm* star Larry David?"

We both whipped around. It was Jagger Wardlow.

Yet another plan out the window.

The tech CEO's eyes were again hidden behind sunglasses, but there was no mistaking the wolfish smirk for anything other than utter contempt. We'd lost the element of surprise. He was sweating profusely. What bothered me the most, however, was the enormous battle-axe in his hands. An intricate design was etched into the steel, along with a gleaming red jewel. It all looked weirdly familiar.

"It looks like I need to run diagnostics on Ben and Jerry once they return to their charging stations," Jagger said. "You seem to have exploited a weakness in their programming."

The crevices in Bernie's resting grump face deepened, to the point where his bottom lip was trembling. Was that smoke rising from his ears, or just a mirage?

"What's up with the axe?" I said. "Hunting dragons?"

"Oh, this thing?" He spun it in his hands. "It's a real-life replica from *Game of Thrones*. I was chopping wood."

The axe's polished edge caught a ray of light. It was no prop.

The One Percent were truly different from you and me.

"Ben and Jerry told us everything," Bernie bluffed. "Sneaking that autopsy report to us using your drones? Clever. What's your interest in the Ferman Fletcher case?"

Jagger leaned the axe against Bernie's car. I'd been wondering how long he could hold on to it, given that its handle was wider than Jagger's upper arms. "Mr. Fletcher was an associate of mine," he said. "When he spoke, these hick farmers listened. Sometimes, I fear, he could go a little overboard. When I discovered our worksite had been vandalized the same night Mr. Fletcher quote-unquote 'drowned,' I worried someone out there might have developed a vendetta. I did some poking around in the sheriff's department's servers. Would you believe the autopsy report was sitting unread in the sheriff's inbox?"

I believed him. INBOX: ZERO was an urban legend. His email was probably just as much of a mess as everyone else's. Did that justify hacking into the department's files, though?

"What was I supposed to do with the report?" Bernie asked. "You could have taken it directly to the State Police."

"The more intermediaries, the less likely it was that the leak would be traced back to me. I didn't expect the two of you to go full *Knives Out*. If I'd known you were going to continue with this sick fixation on me and my company, I would have gone to the State Police. Then again, there's been a state policeman in Eagle Creek all weekend. They're hardly any better than the sheriff's department."

"If that's truly how you feel," I said, "why not take it to the FBI?"

"You're right," Jagger quipped. "But as I said, I needed an intermediary who would take my concerns seriously. Not these northern rednecks who think flannel is finer than silk. There's just something I admire about the senator. He's honest to a fault. You always know where you stand with him."

"You keep calling these people hicks," Bernie said. "They're hardworking folk. They just want to make a living. Maple syrup is the only thing this town has ever known. How dare you come in here and start flashing your money around like some Silicon Valley colonialist."

"That's the American way, Senator. And obviously I didn't kill my own banker. I do want to know who killed him, though. If they think I'm next, they have another thing coming." He held up the axe. "Defending yourself with lethal force is also the American way, right?"

"C'mon," I told Bernie under my breath. "We should go. The parade starts soon."

"Are we still doing that?" Bernie asked. "I hate to say it, but turnout hasn't been great all weekend. We currently have more suspects for the murder of Ferman Fletcher than people who showed up at our picnic yesterday."

"Please," I said. "It's your last event of the weekend. It's better to show up than give up."

"My father used to say that," Bernie said.

I feigned ignorance, but now that he mentioned it, I realized it was lifted straight from one of the Bernie biographies I'd skimmed for my internship interview. My bad.

"Fine," he said. He turned back to Jagger. "We're not through."

Jagger wasn't the Maple Murderer. The last thing the killer would want to do is draw attention to the autopsy report after the case had already been closed. At least I knew now Rhea hadn't been the one to bury the report. She'd never seen it—it had been sitting in her father's inbox all this time. In fact, it might have been time for the sheriff to retire and for his daughter to take over.

As for the rest of the town, what was done was done. The maple industry would be dragged kicking and screaming into the future, with or without the people of Vermont. Returning to the days of yore was about as likely as CDs making a comeback in the age of streaming. Then again, vinyl sales had exploded in the past several years. None of the geniuses in Big Tech had foreseen that. By the time demand began to surge for record players, there was only one tiny company left with the institutional knowledge to manufacture them. Perhaps the future didn't have to be as cold and heartless as Jagger Wardlow envisioned it. Perhaps the future could be whatever we wanted it to be.

But that was the future.

This was now.

And now, Bernie had a parade to grand marshal.

Chapter 24

Or not.

"Canceled?" I said, trying to keep my voice down and failing miserably. We had just returned to the store. Bernie was upstairs changing, so I was going to have to be the one to break it to him. "What do you mean it's canceled?"

My mother threw her arms up. "Don't shoot the messenger, Crash. It was the mayor's call."

I sat down in the nearest chair and tried not to scream. The dining room was packed. Full capacity: fourteen chairs, fourteen people. One white Lab and one black cat—Selena Gomez, who else?—giving the dog the stink eye. I kept my screaming on the inside so I wouldn't scare away the diners. "I'm totally getting fired," I choked out.

Mom sat next to me and rubbed my back like she used to. "It's not your fault, sweetheart. How about I make you some apple griddlecakes? I just bought some new syrup. The fancy stuff—Grade A Golden."

I sat up and looked at her. "Where did you find it?"

"Everything's Maple finally got some stock in yesterday. It's no-brand stuff. Hopefully, it's not rancid."

Everything's Maple. The Blooming sisters. I had to find Bernie.

"I'll be back for supper," I told my mother. "Save some griddle-cakes for me."

On my way upstairs, I saw Rhea, in uniform, filling her water bottle at the bottling station. She grabbed my arm. "Hey, Crash. Ty told me the two of you talked. Are we cool?"

I almost laughed. Her and my cousin hooking up was far down on my list of concerns. If it were a Google search, it wouldn't have been on the first or even the second page. As long as they were happy, what business was it of mine? Catching murderers was apparently my business now.

"We're cool," I said.

Bernie descended the stairs in his gray suit. He'd even taken the time to put a tie on. I crossed the dining room and met him at the bottom of the stairs. "You might want to loosen the tie," I told him. "I have good news but also bad news."

"Bad news?"

"The mayor canceled the parade. But the good news—"

"She finally decided there was a danger to the public," Bernie said.

"Not exactly," I said. I relayed the extenuating circumstances as my mother had explained them to me. It had all started yesterday evening when Joey's sister McKayla was crowned this year's Maple Queen. (Fist pump!) Her crypto TED Talk had been a hit with the judging committee, and she'd crushed the flannel competition with a checkered Filson Alaskan Guide Shirt. Things took a turn during her acceptance speech, however, when McKayla abdicated the crown in protest, citing the negative effect of pageants on the cognitive and emotional development of young girls. She shouted something about the downfall of the patriarchy, declaring that the "future is female."

I just wished Joey could have been there. He would have been so proud. His parents recorded the whole thing, and once Joey could open his eyes he'd be able to watch it.

The rest of the town, however, was not quite so charmed. In certain corners, yes. And almost everybody believed it was a quarter century too late to be holding beauty pageants, especially ones that focused exclusively on one gender. At the very least, it was time for a Maple King, wasn't it? These were all healthy discussions to have. The trouble was that the Maple Queen traditionally rode on the Champ float with the grand marshal.

"That's me," Bernie said.

"That's you. Here's where it all goes south."

A disagreement broke out amongst the judges and, eventually, the parents of the contestants as to how to crown another Maple Queen. McKayla had been a unanimous pick. There was nothing in the Champ Days bylaws that addressed a situation such as this. The disagreement soon took a physical turn, and Rhea had to fire her gun into the air to break it up. It was, in fact, the first time a law officer had ever fired a gun on duty in Eagle Creek. Nobody was more shocked than she was. "GO HOME AND SLEEP IT OFF," she ordered the town as plaster dusted her strawberry-blond hair, giving her a makeshift crown.

"No wonder it was practically dead in here this morning," Bernie said.

"Everyone gathered here an hour ago and when they couldn't come up with a consensus, they dragged their kids their separate ways."

"I want to meet this girl. McKayla, you said? I need to give her a medal."

I told him I'd see what I could do. "It's the last year they're going to serve beer at the pageant," I said. "Might be the last year for the pageant. If we're lucky."

A table opened up, and Bernie and I grabbed coffee and sat down. "I still don't see why the parade was cancelled," he said.

"Without a Maple Queen, what's the point?"

"What about me?" Bernie said. "Or would they rather have Larry David."

"It's complicated," I said. "But there's good news."

I told Bernie that my mother had found a bottle of the good stuff at Everything's Maple yesterday. Doc's barrel goes missing and suddenly the Blooming sisters are swimming in liquid gold? It was the very definition of suspect. We were close to cracking the case.

"Did you talk to the sisters yet?" he asked.

"We'll wait for people to clear out, first."

"You expecting a scene?"

"We've never seen eye to eye. They're old-school. No children of their own—they believe children should be seen and not heard. They retired here when their husbands passed. That was before I was born."

"May have been before I was born, too," Bernie said.

"I wouldn't doubt it. Whatever you do, don't make them angry. They're like the Hulk: you won't like them when they're angry."

"The wrestler?" He coughed. "I don't keep up on any of that stuff."

"He's a comic book character. One of the Avengers?"

"Talk to my grandkids," he said. "Who has time for comic books or movies when the climate crisis is accelerating at such an exponential rate? Besides Senator Leahy."

That's when I noticed the Blooming sisters were watching us from across the dining room. As soon as our eyes met, they hurriedly packed up their knitting and made their way for the door. "I think we've got a couple of birds trying to fly the coop," I said.

Bernie rose. "People say that all the time, but unless you've had a coop, you have no idea what it's like. No idea."

I told him I'd meet him out front, and went to pay for our coffee. My mother greeted me with a smile from behind the register. She looked tired. I'd never noticed the lines around her eyes before. In my mind, she was and would forever be ageless.

"Bernie doesn't seem too upset about the parade," she said.

"It's more of a problem for me than for him. I've never failed at anything before. This whole weekend has been a mess, and it's all going to be pinned on me."

"I should have let you fail more," she said, accepting my money without a fight. That was a first. I wasn't sure I liked this part about being an adult—offering to pay a bill and not having either her or my boss say they'd cover it. "You know what I see, though? I don't see a failure. I see my daughter. Twenty-three years old and working side by side with one of the most powerful men in this country."

"This weekend, yes, but this is the first time—"

She placed a finger over my lips. "There's something else I never taught you. How to take a compliment. Now go. He's banging on the window and waving at you . . . Nope, there he goes. He's running down the street. Wow, he's a fast one."

Chapter 25

By the time I caught up to Bernie, he was waiting for me outside the Blooming sisters' gift shop. It was, after all, only a block away from the general store.

"They went inside," he said. "Then they flipped the OPEN sign around on the door. They want to go back to business as usual."

"Think they're onto us?" I asked.

"Only one way to find out," he said, opening the door for me.

When we entered, the sisters looked up from behind the counter. They'd been flipping through Florida travel brochures. Planning their escape? Or had they finally reached the age where New Englanders magically sprout wings and turn into snowbirds?

"Could we help you?" Edwina asked. She had a knitted cardigan on over a knitted sweater.

"I want a bottle of your lightest syrup," Bernie said. "Barrel-aged, preferably."

The sisters exchanged a worried look. Maude shook her head. "I'm sorry, we can't help you, Mr. Senator. Try next spring. If you join our email list—"

I slapped my hand down on the counter, startling everyone, including myself. "Sorry," I said. "Do you mind checking your storeroom to see if you have anything in back? Word on Main Street is you've got a secret stash on these premises."

Edwina took charge this time. "You'll have to get a warrant if you want to see our storeroom."

Maude put her hand on her sister's shoulder. "Forget it, Edwina. We should have known it was too good to be true."

"What was too good to be true?" Bernie asked.

"We picked up a barrel of some of the lightest syrup we've ever seen," Edwina said. "Almost as good as Doc's, though don't tell him I said that. It was a little too sweet."

"You could tell someone added just a pinch of sweetener," Maude said, holding her thumb and forefinger an inch apart.

"Who did you buy it from?" I asked. I had no idea if they were telling the truth or trying to confuse us. There were two of them, but I couldn't see them moving a barrel of that size by themselves. At the very least, they had a partner.

"We weren't supposed to ask where it came from," Edwina said. "We were supposed to keep it hush-hush."

Bernie shook his head in disappointment. "It could have been from Canada, for all you know. Canada!"

The sisters shot a glance at the storeroom, and then back at each other. After living and working together for so long, they could carry on entire conversations with each other with only their eyes. "Follow us," Maude finally said, speaking for the both of them.

They flipped the sign back around in the window and led us into the storeroom. The oak barrel was sitting in the middle of the room, surrounded by boxes. By itself, it looked unremarkable. Nobody who didn't traffic in rare syrups would have known the true value of what was inside. Even the cheapest syrup was, on a gallon-to-gallon basis, worth more than crude oil.

"Who left the back door open?" Edwina said, staring knitting needles at her sister. "There's only two of us who work here, and it wasn't me."

"It wasn't me, either," Maude said.

Through the open back door, I could see a monstrous black pickup parked in the gravel driveway. I glanced back to the barrel. There was a key ring lying on top of it. I had a sinking feeling in the pit of my stomach like I'd just realized I'd forgotten to return a library book by the due date. This was about to get ugly.

A toilet flushed from inside the employee restroom. The mayor stepped out and nearly tripped over her own feet when she saw us. "Looks like the whole gang's here," she said, trying to act casual and failing big-time.

"What are you doing back here?" Edwina hissed.

The mayor glared at her. "How is this 'keeping quiet'? I trusted you. Both of you. Maybe I should have the board take another look at Maplewood's application. How would you like that?"

Edwina's face went white as Vermont cheddar. "You wouldn't."

The mayor stepped closer to her, getting right up in her space. "Afraid of a little competition, are you?"

"It looks to me like she's not the one who's afraid, Mayor," Bernie said. "It looks to me like you were having second thoughts about whatever deal you'd struck with the sisters. Maybe you saw Detective Blackheart out at Doc's yesterday, and felt the heat being turned up. A stolen barrel of Grade A syrup? That's a felony in Vermont. What were you going to do, roll the barrel out of here? How were you planning to get it onto your truck?"

Before Mayor Seeley could defend herself, Maude piled on. "You can't just come in here as you please," she said. "And you most definitely will not be taking that syrup back. That's our ticket to Florida this winter."

"Nobody's taking the syrup anywhere, unless it's back to Doc's," Bernie said.

"It-it can't be Doc's," Maude stammered. "It can't be. Tammy, you said—"

"The barrel is Doc's," Mayor Seeley snapped. "The syrup is . . . well, it's complicated. He doesn't want his name on it for reasons I'm not at liberty to divulge."

"Was that deal struck before or after Mr. Fletcher died?" I asked.

"Enough!" the mayor shouted. "I had no idea anyone cared that much about one dead, lousy banker. Whoever drowned him in that syrup did this community a favor."

There was a long silence.

Finally, Bernie spoke up. "Nobody said anything about him drowning in syrup."

The mayor swallowed hard. It was like she was trying to swallow her guilt, but it wouldn't go down.

"What happens when I tap that barrel?" Bernie said, his voice booming like he was at a rally calling for the government to forgive $1.2 trillion in student loan debt. "Even the smallest nose hair would be enough to place Ferman Fletcher's head in that barrel. And then it's only a matter of time while the State Police build their case . . ."

"We've been selling murder syrup?" Edwina said. Maude gasped and swooned into her sister's arms. Luckily, Edwina had just enough muscle on those chicken-leg arms to catch Maude.

I plucked the mayor's keys off the barrel. There was a key fob connected to the key ring, and I wanted to cut off the most obvious escape route for her. "I'm going to hold on to these for now. If you don't mind."

"Do whatever you want," the mayor said. "That seems to be what your generation does. Somebody needs to spank that Wardlow boy."

"He might enjoy that," I said. "So what does Jagger Wardlow have to do with Mr. Fletcher drowning?"

"Everything!" the mayor said. "Ferman was deep in Jagger's pocket. They'd scooped up every maple farm in the county except for a handful. Doc was one of the final holdouts. He would never sell, and Ferman knew it. And that made him mad, oh so mad. It wasn't personal at first, but it became a point of pride for Ferman. Thursday night, I was leaving city hall late and I see Ferman stumbling out of the Moose Knuckle. Looked like he'd had one too many. When he got behind the wheel of his Kia, I thought, *I should stop him before he hurts somebody*. Because that's the type of person I am. A good person."

Bernie cleared his throat. "Continue."

"Ferman turned north onto the highway and floored it. So I followed."

Maude spoke up. "Ferman still lived in that ugly new construction south of town, didn't he?"

The mayor nodded. "I followed him out to Old Critters Lane. He was so far gone he didn't know I was tailing him. I watched him park a hundred yards from Doc's place. He got out and started walking, carrying something in his right hand. My first thought was, he was going to threaten Doc. When I caught up to him, though, I found him behind Doc's cabin. It wasn't a gun. It was a bottle of—"

"—corn syrup," I said excitedly.

"That's right," she said. "Ferman had pried the lid off Doc's reserve barrel and was emptying it in."

Edwina gasped and fainted into her sister's arms. Maude made the catch this time.

Mayor Seeley ignored their histrionics. "Doc would be out of business in a heartbeat if anyone discovered corn syrup in a bottle with his name on it," the mayor went on. "I grabbed the bottle from that vile man, Ferman. He tried to grab it back so I pushed him. I pushed him and he went right into the barrel headfirst. His legs were sticking up in the air, kicking all around."

"You didn't try to help him out?" I asked.

"I thought it might teach him a lesson, choking on his own medicine. I didn't expect him to actually drown. By the time I pulled him out, I realized I might have made an error in judgment. You can put together the rest."

"Where was Doc during all of this?" Bernie asked.

"Asleep. After I loaded Ferman's body into my truck, I went in and woke Doc up. Told him I'd been at my deer camp and saw some hooligans in back of his place. He just about died when he saw the empty bottle of corn syrup and ruined barrel. I told him I could find a buyer for it. He helped me load it up, and that was the last I saw of Doc. He didn't see the body under the tarp in my truck bed, but he guessed Jagger Wardlow had ordered the sabotage operation."

I nodded. "So when you picked us up out that way . . ."

"I was trapping squirrels," she said. "And—okay, maybe I happened to see Joey Blackheart and the fire truck and all the hullabaloo at Doc's. I realized that the sisters wouldn't sell it off as fast as I'd have liked. I needed to dispose of the barrel, because there was too much heat."

"You've been very forthcoming," Bernie said, and I agreed. She'd been too forthcoming. Unnervingly so. I didn't like it.

"I've been waiting for sirens, but I haven't heard any," she said. "There are no helicopters overhead. No SWAT team kicking the windows in."

"Are you disappointed?" I asked.

"No, I just wanted to make sure I wasn't going to get shot if I ran for it."

And with that, the mayor bolted into the shopfront, leaving the storeroom door flapping in her wake. As she dashed past the register, she snatched the sisters' keys from the counter. Nobody moved at first, shocked by her swiftness and baffled at the audacity of her plan. By the time we reached the gravel lot, she had already started the sisters' golf cart and was backing out.

"Where does she think she's going?" Bernie said, watching Mayor Seeley turn out onto the highway.

Edwina and Maude poked their heads out from between us. "Florida," they said together, with dreamy looks in their eyes. Or possibly cataracts.

I called the general store. My mother picked up on the third ring.

"Mom, it's me," I said. "Is Rhea still there? Tell her this is important. There's a fugitive headed south out of town on a golf cart."

"That sounds like Champ Days, alright," my mom said. "But Rhea's not here. She left with the other deputies. They're all out at the Maplewood sugar shack. They found Doc. He climbed one of the tallest maples in the woods they've been clearing. It was supposed to be a protest, to draw attention to what's happening. Trouble is, he's stuck up there. Been up there for a few days, apparently, without anybody noticing. Nobody heard him, either. He lost his voice yelling for help."

That all tracked with what I knew about Doc. I was glad he was alive. I told my mother that if she could reach anyone in the sheriff's department, to text me back.

"Well," I said after ending the call. "Doc's alive, but there's a rescue operation under way. Long story. Unfortunately, that means there isn't any law enforcement immediately available. It looks like it's just you and me, Senator."

And with that, we were off.

Except Bernie couldn't find his keys. He patted himself down. "Must be back in my room," he grumbled.

"Ahem." I dangled the mayor's keys in his face. "Can you drive stick?"

Chapter 26

The outcome of the chase was never in doubt. Despite Mayor Seeley's head start, we caught up to the stolen golf cart in less than a minute. We kept pace with her, inching side by side down the highway well under twenty-three miles per hour. Bernie had to wave several cars around us. Judging by the lewdness of the insults hurled our way, most of the drivers were from Boston. It wasn't the parade Eagle Creek wanted, but it was the one we deserved.

Just as the world's slowest car chase was approaching the edge of town, the golf cart sputtered and died. Bernie pulled onto the shoulder in front of the stalled vehicle. In the rearview, I watched the mayor cross the road, dodging traffic on foot. She was headed down a ravine toward the lakeshore.

"Should we follow her?" I asked Bernie.

He tapped his fingers on the wheel. "No."

"So . . . are we going to follow her?"

"Definitely."

It didn't take long to reach her. She'd fled to the end of a private dock and simply run out of room. There was a jet ski tied up to the dock, but without any keys she hadn't been able to start it. There was no escape. All we had to do now was wait for Rhea or one of her deputies to arrive. How many emergency responders did it take to rescue one man stuck in a tree?

"There's nowhere to run," Bernie shouted from the metal steps leading down to the dock.

Mayor Seeley didn't turn. She was staring out across the lake. "Who said I was running?" she said into the light breeze. "It's just a nice day for a drive in the country."

The dock wasn't long, only ten feet or so. It bobbed up and down with the water, making it hazardous to walk on. Bernie and I saw this and made the mutual decision to stick to the metal staircase.

"Are you going to tell us why you did it?" Bernie said.

The mayor looked over her shoulder. "I already confessed. Or did you forget?"

I shot Bernie a quizzical look. What was he driving at?

"You mentioned whoever killed Fletcher did Eagle Creek a favor," Bernie said. "You wouldn't have lifted a finger to stop him unless it benefitted you personally. With all the money Maplewood has flooded this town with, you expect us to believe you weren't getting a cut? Siding with Doc seems like a poor financial decision."

Tamara's gaze was still fixed on the water. Small whitecaps were beginning to form as the wind picked up. Whether it was her future or past in the lake, I didn't know. It was clear that she wasn't entirely here with us. She was someplace far away from Eagle Creek, where Bernie's voice was a distant echo.

"When I moved to Eagle Creek, it was a small township," the mayor said. "Not even a hundred residents. Then it exploded, as more flatlanders moved to Vermont. In just a couple of years, the population ballooned to a thousand. When Eagle Creek crossed the two thousand mark, it triggered a clause in the town's bylaws that required a mayoral election. Which I won, of course."

Only beating the goat on a technicality, I thought, but now was no time to rub it in.

"The population was steady for many, many years. Until the downturn in the maple industry. Maplewood Springs came to town and have been hollowing Eagle Creek out, farm by farm. Replacing workers with robots. If we lose another hundred citizens, the population will drop to under two thousand."

"And you'll be out of a job," Bernie said.

She wiped a tear from her eye. "Worse," she said. "I'll be demoted to city clerk. No more state council meetings. No more ribbon-cutting ceremonies. Just paperwork. Endless paperwork."

"You forgot who elected you," Bernie said. "It was the people. Public office isn't about you. It's about them. The people of Eagle Creek deserve better."

There was no malice in his gruff voice.

There was no empathy, either.

An uncomfortable silence descended over the dock. The only sound was the wind in my ears. I lowered my voice. "You think a jury will convict her?" I asked Bernie. "She may not be as altruistic as she claims, but Mr. Fletcher was a banker. If she gets a good lawyer, they'll paint him as a fat cat who was getting rich off the little people of this town. Throw in the way he was putting the screws to homeowners, and she could come out of this a hero to some."

"Remember, though, that she's a politician," Bernie said. "The only thing people hate more than a fat-cat banker is a corrupt politician."

I nodded. "Facts."

Bernie swatted at a swarm of gnats. The tiny insects dispersed and came right back together, circling Bernie's head. They had it in for him.

"The justice system in this country is far from perfect," he continued, still swatting away. "It too often seems like it has little to do with 'justice.' The tragic reality is that the United States of America has more people in prison than any other country. But make no mistake: Tamara Seeley deserves to be behind bars for what she's done."

The spot where the mayor had been sitting was empty.

"We have a small problem," I said, pointing to the end of the dock.

He spun around. "You're kidding me."

While we'd been chatting about the justice system and its failings, Tamara had evaluated her options and decided to swim for it. She knew how cold the water was this time of year. Did she really think she had a better chance with the elements than with the justice system? What had Joey said about the water temp right now? *Even if you're a decent swimmer, your arms and legs will eventually go numb.*

The mayor surfaced ten feet out from where she'd gone in, spitting out water and gasping for air before going back under. Bernie and I raced to the end of the dock. The water, usually clear, was dark and murky today.

"Mrs. Mayor!" I yelled. Bernie had removed his shoes and was working off his socks before I noticed what he was up to. "You're not going in after her," I said. "Rhea or one of the other deputies will be here soon. They're trained for this sort of thing. They'll have a rope, or—"

"They're not here now," Bernie said, unzipping his slacks. "And I don't see a lifeguard on duty."

I was about to scream at him to cover up when I saw that he had on a pair of long-board swim trunks. They were brightly decorated with lobsters.

"You were wearing swim trunks today just on the off chance you had spare time to take a dip in the lake?" I asked.

"I forgot to pack enough boxers and this was all your mother's store had in stock," he said. "Lucky break for the mayor."

Lucky break for us all, I thought.

He dove off the end of the dock, performing a perfect dive into Lake Champlain with minimal water resistance and splash. The pink bottoms of his feet went under last, leaving me all alone on the swaying dock.

Bernie had been a decorated high school athlete. He might have traded his letterman's jacket for a gray suit jacket from Men's Wearhouse, but he could still swim like a greased otter. A chill went up my spine just watching him, imagining how cold the water was. Not that a summer rescue would have been any easier. Lake Champlain was a harsh mistress, with surprising drop-offs and invisible undercurrents close to the shore. Heavy water, the old-timers would say. Bernie's skills would be put to the test.

He surfaced not far from the dock, treading in place, searching for some sign of the mayor.

"There!" I shouted, pointing at the mayor, struggling to keep her head above water. She was drifting farther and farther from shore.

Bernie formed a V with his hands and swam for her. He cut a path through the water with frightening speed. Yet he couldn't keep pace with her. Bernie wasn't catching up fast enough.

There were two rescue rings tied to the jet ski. Bernie had overlooked them, and now he was too far from the dock to reach it if I threw one to him. Unless . . .

I lowered myself onto the jet ski and undid the rope tethering it to the dock. There were no keys in the ignition, but I didn't need any. It's like I said: stealing golf carts was a rite of passage in Eagle Creek. I wasn't much of a delinquent in the traditional sense, but I'd had a little fun. As my dad would say if he were here, *If you can hotwire a golf cart, you can hotwire a jet ski.*

A few crossed wires later and the engine thrummed to life for me. The owner had been kind enough to leave a quarter of a tank of gas. Joey had told me not to do anything reckless until he got back. These were extenuating circumstances, however.

I gave it some gas and it shot forward. I gripped the handlebars tight as a plume of water shot high into the air behind me, dissipating in the wind and misting me. Goosebumps rose on the back of my neck.

I motored straight past Bernie, nearly clipping him in the process. "I'll be back for you!" I yelled into the wind as the jet ski sprayed my boss. The list of apologies I owed him was growing.

I steered toward where I'd last seen the mayor, and then let up on the gas. Idling in place, I scanned the water for some sign of life. "Mrs. Mayor!" I called. "Tamara!"

There—ten feet from me. Bobbing up and down, treading water. How much longer could she last? Bernie was still swimming her way, but he was slowing.

I undid the rings from the jet ski. I dug deep into my bag of tricks, remembering the ring-toss game from Champ Days past.

I whipped one of the rescue rings around, sailing it like a Frisbee on the breeze. The wind took hold of it, as expected. Thankfully, I'd compensated for that and underthrown it—this wasn't my first carnival game. The mayor latched onto it. As she did, however, the rope went taut and trapped my foot in a loop. When I reached down to loosen it, I accidentally hit the gas and toppled headfirst into the frigid water.

I had no time to prepare. The cold hit me all at once, like a thousand pinpricks. I clawed for the surface, but my flailing arms couldn't reach the surface. Was I still upside down? I'd lost all sense of direction. The water was black as a country night. All my flailing had only succeeded in pushing me deeper underwater into darkened limbo. The rope had come off from around my ankle, but oh the price. The depth this far out was between 40 and 120 feet. How far down was I? And how long was the air trapped in my lungs going to last? This was just my luck. The one time I go out on the lake without a life jacket and I end up drowning. Even worse, I was going to die a footnote. I was an intern. A nobody. Fifteen bucks an hour wasn't just a living wage. It would be my dying wage.

And yet. There was one reason, and one reason only, I knew this wasn't the end.

I still had student loan debt.

The universe wouldn't let me off this easy.

Something nudged my side, sending me spinning head over heels. My first thought was a shark testing me to see if I was prey, but of course there weren't any sharks in Lake Champlain. A sturgeon? Whatever it was, it was an absolute honker. My eyes must have been finally adjusting to the low light, because when it closed in on me again we wound up face-to-face. Its head alone was larger than any sturgeon that had ever been pulled out of a freshwater lake. Its long, lean neck extended into the darkness, where a shadowy body the size of a school bus awaited. The creature—nay, the *beast*—cocked its head, examining me with two unblinking, softball-sized black orbs.

It couldn't be real. None of this was real. It was a trick of my oxygen-starved brain, that was all. I was on the verge of losing consciousness. People who survive near-death experiences speak of seeing a long, dark tunnel with a light at the end of it. The light draws them in, closer, closer, until they can make out figures waiting to greet them. Dead relatives, welcoming them to the Great Beyond.

I wasn't being greeted by my great-grandparents.

I was being greeted by Champ.

It was that same lack of oxygen that I blame for what I did next.

I reached a hand out to it. I didn't know if it was carnivorous or not, but I had to touch it. It was too darned cute. I ran my fingertips over the rough, leathery hide of its snout. Instead of shaking me off, it lowered its head and nuzzled my hand like Selena Gomez asking for pets.

Without warning, the beast disappeared into the darkness. I barely had time to question what I'd just seen when it lifted me from beneath with its snout, pushing me up toward the light. With a great splash I broke the surface, gasping for air. By the time I caught my breath, the swirling waters around me had calmed, leaving me alone and adrift on the lake. Had I just joined the ranks of Vermonters who believed in Champ?

"Grab the ring!" a voice shot out.

It was Bernie. He was piloting the jet ski, white hair whipping in the wind. His glasses were still on his face. The mayor was riding double with her arms wrapped tight around the senator's waist.

"Grab it," Bernie repeated, circling me, dragging the flotation ring behind him. I summoned the last remnants of my strength and snagged it. "Now hold on," he said, pointing us toward land. "And try not to drown. It'll ruin your day."

Chapter 27

Bernie left me with the mayor on the shore. She was too weak to stand. The mayor had tried to escape, and Lake Champlain had spit her back up. Our teeth were chattering, but we would live.

After a few minutes, Bernie returned. He'd changed back into his suit and brought us some towels and blankets from the B&B. "Deputy Kelly should be here in a few minutes," he said, handing me a pair of striped mittens and his jacket.

I knew better than to ask any questions about the mittens.

A large boat rounded the bend and came into view. It wasn't Eagle Creek's finest.

It was Eagle Creek's worst.

I turned to Bernie. "We did say we weren't done with him."

Jagger anchored the boat a hundred yards from shore. Come any closer, and he risked painting the rocks with the underside of his boat. I'd seen many a flatlander boat smaller than his take a fatal beating.

He lowered himself into a wooden canoe and paddled toward us. Against our better judgment, we helped him tie up the canoe and steadied it so he could climb out. He was unarmed (no battle axes, broadswords, or crossbows).

He looked at the mayor, then at us. "You've unmasked the killer," Jagger said, clutching his chest with mock sincerity. Of course he'd heard the 911 call I'd placed, to let emergency services know we'd also need an ambulance and not just a paddy wagon. Tamara was still shivering. "That's a big weight off me," Jagger said. "If there's anything I can do for you . . ."

"You can hire some union workers for your projects," Bernie said. "Better yet, you can head back to Silicon Valley."

Jagger laughed. "I was thinking more like . . . a year's supply of maple syrup."

My mouth fell open. "You. Creep."

Bernie placed a hand on my shoulder to settle me down. "I have to agree with Crash," he said. "Even though I go through a couple bottles a month, that's still a wretched offer. Also, my maple cellar is stocked full. I could survive on what I've got down in Burlington through a couple more pandemics."

The bearded CEO shrugged. "I suggest you retire to your maple cellar, then. I own these hills. I own this town. I own—"

Mayor Seeley tackled him, driving him to the ground. They rolled around on the bed of dirty ground and dead leaves before Jagger finally extricated himself. He jumped to his feet and backed away from the mayor. She was on her knees and breathing heavily. It appeared that had been her last gasp of energy, but we really needed to keep a better eye on her. In my defense, at least, this was the first pseudo-citizen's arrest I'd ever attempted.

"You don't own this town," Tamara said, slumping to a seated position. "This is my town. You'll have to take it from my cold . . . dead . . . hands . . ." Her voice trailed off.

"Please," he begged, "this is too sad to watch. You're harshing my mellow."

Harshing my mellow. Where had I heard that phrase?

I snapped my fingers. "Cannon Cove!"

Both Jagger and Bernie looked at me like I was high. Except I wasn't the one who was high. Behind those sunglasses, Jagger's eyes were almost assuredly bloodshot.

I'd misread him. He wasn't eccentric. He was just really, really high all the time. He was the world's richest stoner, giving away tie-died hoodies and swinging battle-axes in the forest. Why would the world's richest stoner plant his flag in Vermont? It had nothing to do with maple syrup.

"He's not building something in the hills around Eagle Creek," I said. "He's planting something. Marijuana. All of the maple farms are outside city limits, so he'll be able to skirt the town's ban on cultivation."

Jagger wasn't laughing now. He was used to being on offense. Now that he was being forced to play defense, he was out of his comfort zone. He'd never had to play from behind.

"Were you after the Vermont Country Shed, too?" I asked him, pressing my case. "Mr. Fletcher was trying to shake down my mother, same as he was doing to Doc."

"The board must have denied his request to build a new store in town," Bernie said. "Tamara thought he was going to build a gift shop in direct competition with Everything's Maple. His only option, then, would be to buy an existing building zoned for business use. That would explain why Fletcher was pressuring your mother, Crash. What was Jagger going to turn it into, a dispensary? This was never about maple syrup, was it?"

Jagger pulled his hair with both hands. "Maple syrup, maple syrup, maple syrup. Does anyone around here ever think of anything else?" He looked at us with disgust, shaking his head slowly. "Here's a truth bomb: an acre of sugar maples will net you five hundred dollars a year. Do you know what an acre of cannabis will net you? A hundred thousand. But don't worry. I'm keeping the sugar shack up and running, along with one or two of the maple farms. Have you ever tried . . . cannabis-infused maple syrup?"

If Edwina and Maude were here, they would have both fainted at the same time.

"What about all that talk the other day about climate change?" Bernie said. "Clear-cutting these hills will alter the environment in irreversible ways. What do you think is going to happen to the animals in these hills? If there's even one endangered bird—"

"Why do you think I chose to start with Eagle Creek?" Jagger said. "There aren't any endangered animals that call these woods home. There's barely any people that call this place home."

"What about the fish?" Bernie said. "Clear-cutting is going to create runoff into the lake. The freshwater sturgeon—"

"—were removed from the endangered species list last year. They've made a tremendous comeback in these waters. In fact, every animal in the lake has a healthy breeding population."

"Not every animal," I said. Now it was my turn to smirk. "You forgot about Champ."

It took a moment to register with Bernie, but he was picking up what I was throwing down. "No matter how comprehensive your surveys, Wardlow, I doubt you looked into the impact on our little lake monster," he said.

Jagger stopped laughing. "This is a joke, right?"

A fire had been lit in Bernie's eyes. "Do I believe there's a pos-sibility that a prehistoric sea serpent is swimming around Lake Champlain? An *endangered* prehistoric sea serpent that measures fifty to seventy-five feet in length?" He cleared his throat. "You bet your skinny jeans I do, mister."

"Will you go on record saying that?" Jagger asked, pulling his phone out. "The only thing kookier than a socialist is a socialist who believes in the Loch Ness Monster."

"Three things," Bernie said, stabbing a finger at Jagger. "I'm a democratic socialist, and I'm not going to apologize for it. Two: I never said I believed in Champ. I said I believed that the existence of such a creature is within the realm of possibility. If a pathologi-cal liar like Donald Trump can be elected president of the United States, I'm not discounting anything. No matter how absurd."

"You said three things. That's only two."

"I was catching my breath, hold on," Bernie said. "I just swam a hundred yards in the open water, so give an old man a break." Bernie cleared his throat again. It sounded like he was working on a hairball. "Use your little phone machine to look something up for me. There's something you need to read in the Vermont House records. From the 1982 session, I believe. Bill H.R. 19."

The mayor broke into a coughing fit. Bernie slapped her on the back and a minnow flew out of her mouth and landed at Jagger's feet. He kicked it away.

"You want me to read this bill right now?" Jagger said, scowling.

Bernie pointed a finger at him. "Right now."

Jagger did a quick internet search. He read what he found out loud. "H.R. 19 . . . a bill classifying the lake monster identified as 'Champ,' or '*Champtanystropheus*,' as an endangered species." He glared at the screen. "Is this a joke? Anyone can edit Wikipedia. Even you, I bet."

"House of Representatives records that far back aren't online, but you and I can go down to the records office in Montpelier first thing tomorrow," Bernie said.

"What's your point?" Jagger asked.

Now it was Bernie's turn to smirk. The smirking was contagious. "If you move forward clearing these hills, you're potentially affecting the habitat of an endangered species. That falls under the jurisdiction of the Marine Fisheries Service—and you know how slow these government bureaucrats can be. I hear they've got a backlog going back eighteen months. Staffing shortages."

Jagger's mellow having been significantly harshed, he lowered himself into his canoe and retreated to the comfort of his big boat. The onus would be on Maplewood Springs to prove their terraforming wasn't a threat to Champ, whose eating and mating habits were complete unknowns. Until they could do the necessary surveying—which could take years—it appeared the maple trees around Eagle Creek had themselves a temporary reprieve.

"So that's a real bill?" I asked Bernie.

"More or less," he said. "At the time, it was mostly a PR stunt cooked up by some hotshot young mayor to boost tourism. Must have been a three-martini lunch that day, because the House not only agreed to consider it, they voted to approve it. If Wardlow wants to pursue this in court, he's going to have to find a judge willing to consider the intent behind the resolution. The actual wording of it, however, is unambiguous. Champ isn't to be messed with."

"You've read the entire thing, then."

"Read it?" Bernie said, standing tall and proud at the edge of the lake. "I wrote the damn bill."

Chapter 28

"We won," I said to Bernie as we made our way back to the highway. "Why does it feel like we've just kicked the can down the road?"

"Sometimes, that's all you can do," he said. "I ran track in high school. Long-distance. We had others on my team that were sprinters. They were faster than me—for a short distance. Fifty, a hundred meters. But I kept kicking that can—my exhaustion—down the track, and eventually they fell away. I'm not saying that's what our friend here is going to do, but the longer we can play this game, the better our chance of winning."

"Not everyone plays by the rules, though," I said. "The bad guys always have an upper hand."

"Are you telling me you always play by the rules? Ms. Bandi-loot?"

I winced. There was nothing to say, so I said nothing.

He laughed. "Your username went over my head, but you wouldn't believe the background check folks. They're very thorough."

"You never said anything during the interview."

"It didn't have anything to do with your job. Your college transcripts, your references—all of it was impeccable. You're a better student than I ever was, I'll give you that. Want to know the only thing that gave anyone pause? It was that you were from Vermont."

"You're kidding."

He shook his head. "Lana was worried you might be some stalker who'd followed me from the Green Mountain State to Washington. When you gave me that bottle of Doc's, she was convinced of it."

"She's all over me, for every little thing."

"Don't take it personally," Bernie said. "She's just trying to protect me. Lot of leeches in the swamp. They'll bleed you dry if you're not careful."

Everything was on the table, and . . . nothing had changed. Nothing, and everything. Because a weight had been lifted from my chest. I could finally breathe again. This was what relief tasted like, to not have that gnawing anxiety in the back of your mind that everything you'd worked so hard for, for so long, was about to go up in flames.

"Nobody's perfect," he said. He was talking almost more to himself than to me. "Nobody. Not me, not you—not even President Obama." He paused. "Maybe Michelle."

There was a buzz from inside my jacket pocket. I pulled out a phone. It wasn't mine, which confused me for a moment. It was Bernie's phone—I'd forgotten I was wearing his coat. His wife was calling. There was something familiar about her number, however . . .

"I think this is for you," I said, handing it to him.

As he gave her a quick rundown of the day's excitement—leaving out his daring water rescue—I found the business card in my wallet, the one with the fixer's number.

It was Jane's number.

Of course it was.

At least the weekend was over. The Senate was back in session tomorrow; my classes resumed this week. I hadn't needed to call anyone to save me. I still had unanswered questions. Had that really been Champ in the lake? Every minute that elapsed, I became less sure of what I'd seen. It would be some time before I could look back with a clear head. Champ had saved my life, but it was one secret I had to keep to myself. For now.

The other question left unanswered was about my letter of recommendation. Lana wasn't going to be happy with me, but I didn't need Lana, did I? She was Bernie's gatekeeper. I had Bernie right here. If I asked, he would probably sign it. Of that I was ninety-three percent sure. With Bernie, I'd come to understand there was always a margin of error, no matter how certain you were of what he would do.

Except I couldn't ask him. Back in Washington, everybody wanted something from him—an autograph, a selfie, an endorsement. We'd built a rapport this weekend, odd as that sounds. I didn't want to be "that guy."

There was another buzz, this time from my handbag. A text from Lana.

The parade was canceled?! Why did I learn about this on Twitter instead of from you?

I bit my lip. *Been busy,* I texted back. *Long story.*

Her reply was almost instantaneous, as if she'd already had it composed.

If the "long story" doesn't end with Bernie getting on his 7:10 flight as scheduled, don't bother coming back to the office again.

I contemplated chucking my phone into Lake Champlain. The stress was getting to be too much. It wasn't just Lana, it was DC. It was school. The need to be perfect. Didn't Lana know that I was harder on myself than she could ever be? I held myself to high standards because I wanted to succeed where so many others had failed. Failure, however, was guaranteed in politics. Nobody won forever. Bernie had failed to win the Democratic presidential nomination. Twice.

My mother was right. If I never failed, I wasn't challenging myself.

Huh. Sometimes, parents can be right. Yet another unwelcome realization that I'd grown up since leaving home.

We loaded ourselves into Bernie's Subaru, which he'd picked up when returning to the B&B. "I'm getting hungry," he said. "Do you think Mrs. Bowers ever finished making that mac and cheese?"

I raised an eyebrow. "It does sound good. She might not be so accommodating after we pulled that Irish goodbye on her this morning."

"Then where would a man find a decent chowder around here?"

I checked the time on the dash. 5:08. There was just enough time to shower, pack, and get Bernie to the airport on time. There wasn't time to eat anything that wasn't grab-n-go. Clam chowder wasn't exactly something you could eat on the road.

"We're a little crunched for time," I said. "We smell like lake water, and your flight leaves in two hours. Might need to find something at the airport."

He waved me off. "I looked at the Senate schedule tomorrow. I'm not really feeling it."

Frankly, I wasn't really feeling it either. What I wanted was a nice home-cooked meal, some family time around the crackling fireplace in the general store's dining room, and a nice, long bath.

There was no bathtub at my apartment, so it wasn't a difficult decision.

I put my phone in airplane mode. It wasn't as satisfying as tossing it into Lake Champlain, but I was still paying it off. Only twenty-six monthly installments left and then I could upgrade.

"Well," I said, returning my attention to Bernie, "you're staying at a bed-and-breakfast with the best New England clam chowder in town. It's also the only clam chowder in town. We could check out the food trucks again, but I doubt you'll find anything better than my mother's."

He rubbed his chin. "I'm done eating at restaurants on wheels."

"You finally come around on the greenhouse gas emissions?" I asked.

"The poutine didn't sit right with me. It got me thinking, though, with the food poisoning outbreak in Burlington. Who's keeping an eye on these out-of-town food trucks? Make everyone sick in Eagle Creek one day, set up on North Hero the next. Local health departments can't keep up. Online review sites are rigged. It's the Wild West."

"You should write your senator."

He snorted. "I hear that guy doesn't even answer his own mail. Has his interns do it."

"I hear his interns are more than capable."

"I hear that, too," he said, pulling into the general store parking lot.

Whenever someone finds out I interned for THE Bernie Sanders, they always ask the same question: *What's he REALLY like?* I usually say that with Bernie, what you see is what you get.

That's because when I tell them the truth—that he's not just a politician, he's also a damn fine sleuth—they never believe me. Would you?

Epilogue

Two months later.

Outside the Vermont Country Shed, fat snowflakes were just beginning to fall. A nor'easter was blowing in, bringing freezing temperatures and a lot of the white stuff. They were saying a foot in town, two or three in the hills by this afternoon. And that was on top of the several feet still piled up already from the previous week.

It was ten thirty and all eight parking spaces were taken. Ben—or was it Jerry?—lifted off from the back door with a grocery bag in its clutches. Jagger's robotic personal assistants had decided to stay in town after their boss sold off Maplewood Springs to a consortium of local farmers led by (who else?) Doc McGilliam. Mom couldn't afford to pay them, but she did give Ben and Jerry nights and weekends off. So that was something. Selena Gomez, however, wasn't on board. She hissed at them incessantly. The only other thing that got her dander up like this was the vacuum cleaner. Which gives you some idea of the hurdles AI technology still faces—the Turing test is nothing compared to feline intuition.

Meanwhile, a horde of locals was snapping up milk, bread, and maple syrup like it was the zombie apocalypse. My mother was behind the counter, under siege. Tyler was working more hours these days, but had the day off. Even if my mother could have hired another worker, I think she secretly enjoyed doing everything herself. In that way, we were more alike than I'd ever imagined.

I waved to her and slipped upstairs to drop my bags off in my room. My old room, Ed Sheeran drapes and all. It wasn't locked—this time, my mother had been expecting me. Kids only surprise their parents with unannounced visits in bad TV movies. When your mother has turned your old room into a B&B, arriving unannounced isn't even an option. You need to book weeks in advance.

There was a red envelope on the nightstand. Addressed to me, in care of the store, and postmarked last week in Burlington. No return address, but it didn't need one. Bernie's penmanship was one of a kind, just like him. Plus, the only other person I really knew in Burlington these days was Vermont Department of Corrections inmate number 62389. Otherwise known as Tamara Seeley. She and I weren't exactly pen pals.

The last time I'd talked to the senator had been two months ago, when he dropped me off at the train station in Burlington following our adventure. I'd texted Lana to let her know I wouldn't be returning to the office. *You can't fire me because I quit.* Of course, she didn't know the "long story" I'd promised her. She didn't know just how involved Bernie and I had been in the Maple Murderer case. All Lana knew was how the story had ended: with Bernie flying out of Vermont twenty-four hours past his scheduled departure time. Trying to explain the whole murder mystery thing would have only deepened the hole I was in with Lana. I returned to bartending after she let me go.

I still had Bernie's number. Why hadn't I called him? I suppose a part of me agreed with Lana. It had only taken me an hour to break the first rule of Bernie Club. What if something had happened to the senator on my watch?

Back to the card. The front featured an illustration of a grumpy Bernie in reindeer antlers. It was based on a screenshot that had been passed around as a meme a few years back. "I AM ONCE AGAIN WISHING YOU HAPPY HOLIDAYS," it read. This had to be Jane's doing—no way would Bernie have picked this out himself. The inside inscription was less irreverent, and more Bernie-like. "As we celebrate the holiday season, let us rededicate ourselves to a world of peace—and economic, social, racial, and environmental justice."

Underneath Bernie's and Jane's signatures, he'd added a personal message in his unmistakable scrawl:

> *P.S. I left behind my phone charger—if your mother still has it, can you mail it to me? Just send it postage due. All you need is my name and Burlington. Gary down at the post office will get it to me.*

There was something else in the envelope, too. A stiff paper folded into quarters. I unfolded it. It was a letter on official Sanders office letterhead. "To whom it may concern," it began. "If you do not hire Crash Robertson, you are making a huge mistake. Let me repeat: a HUGE mistake."

Best. Letter. Of. Recommendation. Ever.

The snow was really coming down now. The closest DC ever came to a white Christmas was cloudy gray. Although there was one year we'd had a few flurries. Not for the holidays, but for Inauguration Day. The enduring image of Bernie from that day—bundled up and cross-legged, looking like he had somewhere more important to be—felt like a lifetime ago.

I rifled through the closet and found Bernie's mittens. He'd told me to keep them because he had a million pairs at home. I didn't quite believe it then, and I didn't quite believe it now. What I did know was that I was putting them on and heading outside to play in the snow.

I went down the back steps. I skated in my L.L. Bean boots across icy patches on the sidewalk, with no particular destination in mind. I stuck my tongue out and caught snowflakes, which were big enough to taste. They tasted the same as they had when I'd been a kid: wet and clean. (Not bad but they could have used a little Vermont maple syrup.) I felt carefree in a way I hadn't in a long time. Perhaps it was being back in Eagle Creek, perhaps it was the holidays. Perhaps it was everything all at once. My mother's store had a new lease on life, thanks to an assistance program I'd hooked her up with. On a personal note, I'd finally gotten some real campaign experience. Mayor Seeley's resignation had opened the door for write-in candidates in November's election. I had no interest in being a politician, but I knew someone who did.

Joey wanted to clean up the corruption he'd uncovered in Eagle Creek. Lucky for him, he knew a wannabe campaign manager who was hungry for action. My grades dropped due to the time I put in managing his campaign, but it was worth it when he declared victory.

I was having a little too much fun skating on the sidewalk, because I lost my footing approaching the town square and went butt-first into a tall snowbank. The downtown streets were deserted, as the bank and post office had already closed for the day. Nobody had seen me go down. I was dusting the snow off my jeans when I saw it—a frozen hand, reaching out of the piled-up snow I'd slammed into. I frantically cleared more snow from around it. It wasn't just a hand, but an entire body.

Got your card, I texted Bernie. *Also found another dead body.*

Within seconds, he replied. *In DC or Eagle Creek?*

Do you have to ask? ☺

I'll be there in half an hour, he wrote. Then, before I could respond, he added, *Forgot there's a blizzard. Make that 45 minutes.*

Recipes

FROM THE VERMONT
COUNTRY SHED TO
YOUR HOME

Senate Bean Soup

Total Time: 4 hours
Makes 6 to 8 servings

This easy, crowd-pleasing ham and bean soup has been served for over a hundred years in the Senate Restaurant on Capitol Hill. According to food writer Bernard Clayton, the House of Representatives' rival bean soup "lacks both the prestige and taste of that of the Upper House."

2 pounds dried navy beans
1½ pounds smoked ham hocks
16 cups water
3 cloves garlic, minced
1 onion, chopped
2 tablespoons unsalted butter
Salt and pepper, to taste
Fresh parsley or chives, to garnish (optional)

Rinse the navy beans and run hot water over them until they are slightly whitened.

In a large pot or soup kettle, combine the beans, the ham hocks, and the water. Cover the pot and simmer over low heat for 2 hours, stirring occasionally.

Add the garlic. Continue to simmer until the beans are tender, about 1 hour.

CONTINUED »

Remove the ham hocks and set aside to cool. In a skillet, over medium heat, cook the onion in the butter until lightly browned. When the ham hocks have cooled, dice the meat, discarding the bones and skin. Add the meat and the onion to the soup and bring to a boil.

Season with salt and pepper. Garnish with snippets of parsley or chives (if desired).

Adapted from Senate.gov.

Yankee Pot Roast

Total Time: 4 hours
Makes 4 to 6 servings

This hearty pot roast may be served up alongside mashed potatoes, buttered egg noodles, rice, or prepared riced cauliflower.
And, despite the name, you don't need to be a New Englander to
enjoy it. Although it does taste best on a freezing Sunday evening
during late winter, after a long day hauling steel buckets of sap
from tapped trees to the sugar shack through knee-deep snow.

1 (2- to 3-pound) beef chuck roast

Salt and pepper, to taste

4 tablespoons olive oil

1 large yellow onion, diced

4 garlic cloves, minced

½ teaspoon chopped fresh rosemary, plus 1 sprig

1 teaspoon chopped fresh thyme, plus 1 sprig

1 cup medium-bodied red wine

4 cups beef stock

2 tablespoons tomato paste

3 large carrots, peeled and cut into 2-inch pieces

3 celery ribs, cut into 2-inch pieces

2 cups pearl onions, ends removed and peeled

1 bay leaf

1 sprig fresh rosemary

1 sprig fresh thyme

CONTINUED »

Preheat the oven to 350°F. Position a rack in the lower half of the oven.

Pat chuck roast dry. Season liberally on all sides with salt and pepper.

In a large Dutch oven, over medium-high, heat 2 tablespoons of the olive oil. Add the chuck roast and sear evenly on all sides, about 5 minutes per side, using tongs to turn the roast. Transfer to a plate and set aside.

Lower the heat to medium. Add the remaining 2 tablespoons of olive oil. Add the onion, garlic, chopped rosemary, and chopped thyme. Cook, stirring often, until the onion is translucent, about 6 minutes. Add tomato paste and cook until fragrant.

Add the wine and 1 cup of the beef stock. Bring to a simmer, stirring to scrape the browned bits from the bottom of the pot. Return the browned roast to the pot, adding enough stock to come a little more than halfway up the meat (the amount of stock varies depending on the size of roast). Bring to a simmer.

Cover the pot and transfer it to the oven; cook until the beef is tender, 2 to 2½ hours. Check partway through to be sure that the liquid in the pot is simmering, not boiling, and that there's enough liquid to prevent the meat from drying out.

Remove the pot from the oven. Arrange the carrots, celery, pearl onions, bay leaf, and herb sprigs around the meat. Cover and return to the oven for an additional 20 to 30 minutes, or until the vegetables are tender and a knife slips easily in and out of the meat. Transfer the roast and vegetables to a plate and tent with foil for 15 minutes. Discard the bay leaf and herb sprigs.

Pour drippings through a fine-mesh sieve into a fat separator cup. If you don't have a fat separator cup, you can allow sieved drippings to sit for 5 minutes and then skim the fat from the top. Set the defatted drippings aside.

Arrange the beef and vegetables on a platter and spoon the drippings on top. The beef should be so tender that it breaks easily apart; slicing it before serving may lead to it drying out.

Adapted from NewEngland.com.

Harvest Stuffed Squash

Total Time: 55 minutes
Makes 6 servings

Did you know that livestock accounts for more than 14 percent of greenhouse gas emissions? Vegetarian diets are not only better for your health, they're also better for the planet. To make this autumnal stuffed squash vegetarian friendly, substitute the meat option with a meat substitute. Alternately, the meat option may be omitted entirely—simply double the cooked grain option.

½ cup chopped yellow onion

2 cloves garlic, minced

3 tablespoons extra-virgin olive oil

1 pound ground turkey, ground beef, or bulk pork sausage

Salt and pepper, to taste

6 ounces bag of fresh baby spinach, roughly chopped

1 cup cooked rice, barley, or quinoa

⅔ cup dried cranberries, soaked in hot water and drained

⅔ cup chopped sweet potato, or carrot, steamed until just tender

½ cup grated apple

2 tablespoons chopped fresh flat-leaf parsley

1 teaspoon dried sage

2 tablespoons unsalted butter

½ cup walnut pieces or chopped pecans

½ cup seasoned or plain panko crumbs

3 acorn squash, halved, seeds removed

1 cup low-sodium vegetable stock

CONTINUED »

Preheat the oven to 375°F.

In a medium pan, over medium heat, sauté the onion and garlic in 1 tablespoon of the oil until soft but not browned. Add the meat, season with salt and pepper, and cook until the meat is cooked through. Toss in the chopped spinach and cook until wilted.

Transfer the mixture to a large bowl and add the cooked grain, cranberries, sweet potato, apple, parsley, and sage. Set this stuffing aside.

In a small sauté pan, melt the butter. Add the walnuts and panko and toss to coat. Gently toast, stirring frequently, until lightly browned and fragrant. Set aside.

In a large baking dish or roasting pan, arrange the squash cut-side down and fill the dish with ½ inch of vegetable stock. Bake until the squash shells give with minimal force when poked with a knife, 15 to 20 minutes. Remove the pan from the oven, reserve the remaining stock, and place the squash face-side up in pan. Fill each cavity with ½ to ⅔ cup stuffing and drizzle with the remaining 2 tablespoons oil. Cover tightly the pan with foil.

Bake until the squash are cooked and slightly soft to the touch, about 30 minutes. Check at 15 minutes and, if the edges of the squash are wrinkling or the stuffing appears to be too dry, drizzle with the reserved stock. For the last 5 minutes of baking, remove the foil and top each squash with the panko mixture.

Adapted from Whole Foods Market.

"Feel The Bern!" Maple Sriracha Hot Sauce

Total Time: 15 minutes
Makes 16 to 20 ounces

If you're planning to gift your hot sauce to friends and family this holiday season, you'll need to sterilize the glass jar or bottle for longer shelf life. (Refer to sterilization techniques online.) Instead of allowing the hot sauce to cool, pour it into the jar or bottle while still hot. Cap immediately and use an induction sealer to seal. Cap liners to prevent leakage are optional but recommended. This sounds like a lot of work, but it's worth it to avoid getting hit with lawsuits instead of thank-you cards.

3 tablespoons unsalted butter
1½ cups pure Vermont maple syrup
¾ cup sriracha sauce
¼ cup soy sauce
¼ teaspoon granulated garlic

In a medium saucepan over medium heat, melt the butter.

Add the maple syrup, sriracha, soy sauce, and garlic and stir to combine. Turn the heat to low and simmer for 5 to 10 minutes, stirring often, until just before the sauce reaches the desired consistency. (It will thicken slightly when cooled.) Depending upon the

CONTINUED »

heat level of the sriracha sauce you started with, ventilation, goggles, and gloves may be necessary to avoid eye and skin irritation.

Let cool to room temperature, then transfer to a covered container and refrigerate. The sauce will keep, refrigerated, for up to 3 months.

Adapted from an AllRecipes.com recipe for maple sriracha.

Apple Griddlecakes

Total Time: 30 to 60 minutes
Makes 6 to 8 servings

What's the difference between a griddlecake and a pancake? Nothing, but once you taste your first bite of these seasonal delights, you'll realize the term "pancake" is far too pedestrian for such a divine flat cake. Optional toppings include pure Vermont maple syrup, toasted granola, toasted nuts, whipped cream, and/or butter. Never, ever top griddlecakes with lingonberries.

1½ cups all-purpose flour
1¼ cups whole-wheat flour
¼ cup white granulated sugar
2 tablespoons baking powder
½ teaspoon salt
2 eggs
1½ cups whole milk
1 cup buttermilk
6 tablespoons unsalted butter, melted
3 tablespoons pure Vermont maple syrup
1 teaspoon vanilla extract
1 teaspoon maple extract
1 apple, thinly sliced and tossed in 1 tablespoon
of lemon juice to prevent browning
Ground cinnamon (optional)

CONTINUED »

Preheat the griddle to medium heat.

In a large bowl, mix the all-purpose flour, whole-wheat flour, baking powder, and salt. Set aside.

In a medium bowl, beat the eggs, then add the whole milk, buttermilk, butter, maple syrup, vanilla, and maple extract. Whisk to combine.

Add the wet ingredients to the dry ingredients, stirring quickly to combine. Do not overmix (small, pea-sized lumps are fine). Let sit for at least 10 minutes. Meanwhile, preheat a griddle to medium heat.

Pour the batter onto the griddle using a ¼-cup measuring cup or pancake dispenser, allowing enough space for the batter to spread. Place thin slices of apple onto the surface of each griddlecake and sprinkle with cinnamon while they cook (if desired). Flip the griddlecakes when they start to bubble on one side, about 2 minutes. Cook until golden on both sides.

Adapted from the Vermont's Red Clover Inn pancakes recipe, as cited in The Old Farmer's Almanac.

Poutine

Total Time: 11 hours
Makes 4 servings

This tasty fast-food staple comes to us from Quebec, where the slang word "poutine" translates to "mess." In 2007, Canadian CBC viewers named poutine the tenth greatest Canadian invention of all time, outranking both snowblowers and snowmobiles. The name of the twentieth-century inventor is much disputed. Whoever they were, there's no disputing it took a genius to smother a pile of fries with gravy and cheese curds.

6 medium russet potatoes, unpeeled, scrubbed
1 quart vegetable oil or sunflower oil
1 packet beef gravy mix
2 cups Vermont cheddar cheese curds

Cut the potatoes into sticks or thin slices. In a large bowl of cold water, soak them for at least 8 hours (or overnight) in the refrigerator.

Rinse the potatoes and place in fresh water and line a pan with paper towels. Let the potatoes sit at room temperature for 1 to 2 hours. Drain the fries and lay them the prepared pan and lightly dry to reduce oil splatter.

CONTINUED »

In a deep fryer or deep heavy skillet, heat the oil to 300°F. While the oil is heating, you can begin to prepare the gravy as directed on the packet. Line a plate with a paper towels and set aside.

Working in batches, add the potatoes to the hot oil and cook for 1½ to 2 minutes. Transfer to the prepared plate to drain.

Increase the heat until the oil reaches 375°F. Working in batches, again, fry the potatoes for a second time until lightly golden brown and crispy, 2 to 3 minutes.

Place the fries on a serving platter and sprinkle the cheese curds over them. Ladle the gravy liberally over the fries and cheese. Serve immediately to prevent this soggy mess from getting any soggier.

Adapted from AllRecipies.com.

Vermont Country Shed Clam Chowder

Total Time: 50 minutes
Makes 8 servings

It's not "clam chowder," it's "clam chow-dah."

½ cup unsalted butter
1½ large onions, chopped
¾ cup all-purpose flour
1 quart shucked clams, with liquid
6 (8-ounce) jars clam juice
1 pound boiling potatoes, peeled and chopped
3 cups half-and-half
½ teaspoon chopped fresh dill
Salt and pepper, to taste

In a large kettle or stock pot over medium heat, melt the butter. Add the onions and sauté until translucent (about 12 minutes). Stir in the flour and cook over low heat, stirring frequently, for 2 to 4 minutes. Set aside to cool.

In a separate pot, bring the clams and clam juice to a boil over medium-high heat. Turn the heat to low and simmer for 15 minutes.

CONTINUED »

In a medium saucepan, add the potatoes and cover with water. Bring to a boil and cook until the potatoes are tender, about 15 minutes. Drain and set aside.

Slowly pour the hot clam stock into the butter and flour mixture, stirring constantly. Continue stirring and slowly bring to a boil over medium-high heat. Lower the heat and add the cooked potatoes. Stir in the half-and-half and dill, and season with salt and pepper. Cook until heated through (but do not boil), about 5 minutes.

Adapted from an AllRecipes.com recipe for New England clam chowder.

Vermont Cheddar Mac & Cheese

Total Time: 40 minutes
Makes 4 to 6 servings

Not all Vermont cheddar is made in Vermont, and not all cheddar made in Vermont is Vermont cheddar. Confused? Don't be! "Vermont cheddar" is simply another name for white cheddar. While much of the United States prefers their cheddar cheese dyed yellow, New Englanders love them some white, naturally colored cheddar. Over the years, "Vermont cheddar" became synonymous with white cheddar. And yes, your yellow cheddar is a lie. Deal with it.

1 pound uncooked elbow macaroni

6 tablespoons unsalted butter

3 tablespoons all-purpose flour

½ teaspoon salt

¼ teaspoon pepper or white pepper

¼ teaspoon onion powder

¼ teaspoon garlic powder

1 cup whole milk

1 cup half-and-half

2 ounces cream cheese, softened

8 ounces sharp Vermont cheddar cheese, shredded

8 ounces mild Vermont cheddar cheese, shredded

¼ teaspoon paprika

CONTINUED »

Cook the elbow macaroni noodles as directed on the package. Place in a three-quart casserole dish.

Preheat the oven to 350°F.

In a medium saucepan over medium heat, melt the butter. Turn the heat to low and stir in the flour, salt, pepper, onion powder, and garlic powder. Continue cooking over low heat, stirring constantly until smooth.

Remove the saucepan from the heat. Add the milk and half-and-half to the melted butter mixture, whisking constantly until combined and smooth. Whisk in the cream cheese.

Return the saucepan to low heat, and gradually increase the temperature to medium-high. Stir constantly to prevent the bottom of the pan from scalding until the sauce is thickened and just boiling.

Remove the saucepan from the heat and stir in all but ½ cup of the shredded cheddar cheese until the cheese is melted.

Add the cheese sauce prepared in the saucepan to the cooked elbow macaroni in the casserole dish and stir thoroughly. Bake for 25 minutes.

Remove the casserole dish from the oven. Sprinkle the top with the reserved ½ cup of cheese and paprika, and bake until golden on top, about 5 minutes.

Adapted from Food.com.

Maple Pecan Cookies

Total Time: 1 to 2 hours
Makes 2 dozen cookies

There are many variations of this recipe possible, including substituting walnuts for pecans in the same amount. Have a nut allergy in your family? You can replace the chopped pecans with dried apple bits (again, in the same amount). The apple flavor pairs nicely with the maple. Other dried fruits may be too sweet, however. Especially raisins. Those nasty little wrinkled grapes exist only to ruin perfectly decent cookies.

COOKIES:

1 cup shortening

½ cup unsalted butter, softened

2 cups packed brown sugar

2 eggs

1 teaspoon vanilla extract

1 teaspoon maple flavoring

3 cups all-purpose flour

1½ teaspoons baking powder

1 teaspoon baking soda

½ teaspoon salt

1⅓ cups white baking chips or 8 ounces white baking bar, chopped

¾ cup chopped pecans

CONTINUED »

FROSTING:

¼ cup unsalted butter, softened

1 tablespoon shortening

2 cups confectioners' sugar

1 teaspoon maple flavoring

3 to 5 tablespoons heavy cream

1½ cups pecan halves, lightly toasted

To make the cookies: Preheat the oven to 350°F.

In a large bowl, cream the shortening, butter, and brown sugar until light and fluffy. Add the eggs, one at a time, beating well after each addition. Beat in the vanilla and maple flavoring.

In a medium bowl, combine the flour, baking powder, baking soda, and salt.

Gradually add the flour mixture to the creamed mixture in the large bowl. Mix well, stirring in the baking chips and chopped pecans.

Drop tablespoonfuls of dough 2 inches apart onto ungreased (or parchment-lined) baking sheets. Bake until golden brown, 11 to 13 minutes. Let cool for 3 minutes before moving to wire racks to cool completely.

To make the frosting: In a large bowl, cream the butter and shortening until fluffy. Beat in the in confectioners' sugar, maple flavoring, and heavy cream 1 tablespoon at a time to achieve a light and airy piping consistency.

Frost each cookie with 1 teaspoon of frosting just in the center, using the back of a spoon, a small spatula, or a piping bag. Top each with a lightly-toasted pecan half.

Adapted from TasteofHome.com.

Bernie's Famous Maple Baked Beans

Total Time: 5 to 6½ hours
Makes 12 servings

Instead of boiling them in a Dutch oven, you can soften the beans by soaking them overnight (or for a minimum of 8 hours) in a bowl. Be sure to submerge them thoroughly. In the morning, simply skip to the step where the beans are drained and rinsed. Additionally, legal has asked that it be made clear this recipe is not affiliated with nor endorsed by Senator Bernie Sanders. He refuses to part with his family recipe.

1 pound dried great northern beans
8 ounces thick-sliced bacon strips, chopped
1 large onion, chopped
4 garlic cloves, minced
2½ cups ketchup
¾ cup packed dark-brown sugar
½ cup pure Vermont maple syrup
¼ cup yellow mustard
2 tablespoons Worcestershire sauce
½ teaspoon salt
¼ teaspoon coarsely ground pepper

CONTINUED »

Sort the beans and rinse with cold water. Place the rinsed beans in a Dutch oven with enough water to cover the beans by 2 inches. Bring to a boil, boiling for 2 minutes. Remove the Dutch oven from the heat, cover and let stand until the beans are softened, about 1 hour.

Drain and rinse the beans, discarding any liquid. Add 6 cups water and bring to a boil. Reduce the heat to low. Cover and simmer for 1 to 1½ hours or until the beans are almost tender, 1 to 1½ hours. Line a plate with paper towels and set aside.

Preheat the oven to 325°F.

In a large skillet, cook the bacon over medium heat until crisp. Transfer to the paper–towel lined plate with a slotted spoon. Drain, reserving 2 tablespoons of the bacon fat in the pan.

Cook the onions in the reserved bacon fat over medium heat, until tender, stirring frequently. Add the garlic and cook for 1 minute. Stir in the ketchup, brown sugar, maple syrup, mustard, Worcestershire sauce, salt, and pepper.

Drain the beans, reserving the cooking liquid. Place the beans in an ungreased three-quart baking dish. Stir in the onion mixture and bacon. Cover and bake until the beans are tender and reach the desired consistency, stirring every 30 minutes, f.or 2½ to 3½ hours. Add the reserved cooking liquid as needed.

Adapted from Taste of Home Favorites—25th Anniversary Edition.

Apple Cider Donuts

Total Time: 35 minutes
Makes 12 to 16 donuts

Making these donut-shop-worthy donuts requires special equipment, such as a stand mixer with a paddle attachment (aka a "flat beater") and two six- or eight-cavity donut pans. But as soon as you smell them baking, you'll forget all about what they cost you. Until you get your credit card statement.

Nonstick cooking spray
1¾ cups all-purpose flour
2 teaspoons ground cinnamon
1 teaspoon salt
½ tablespoon baking powder
¼ teaspoon grated nutmeg
1 cup unsalted butter, at room temperature
¾ cup packed light brown sugar
¾ cup granulated sugar
2 eggs, at room temperature
1 teaspoon vanilla extract
½ cup apple cider, at room temperature

Preheat the oven to 350°F.

Lightly grease two six- or eight-cavity donut pans with nonstick spray and set aside.

CONTINUED »

In a medium bowl, whisk together the flour, 1 teaspoon of the cinnamon, the salt, baking powder, and nutmeg. Set aside.

In the bowl of a stand mixer fitted with the paddle attachment, cream 10 tablespoons of the butter with the brown sugar and ¼ cup of the granulated sugar on medium speed until light and fluffy, 3 to 4 minutes. Add the eggs one at a time and mix until well incorporated after each addition, scraping the bowl as necessary. Beat in the vanilla extract.

Add the flour mixture to the creamed butter mixture. Mix on low speed until incorporated. With the mixer running, add the apple cider in a slow, steady stream and mix to combine. Scrape the bowl well to make sure the batter is all the same consistency.

Spoon the batter into the prepared donut pans, filling them about two-thirds of the way. Filling a donut pan with batter can get messy! Instead of just spooning it in, you can either use a disposable piping bag or—a little cheaper—a resealable plastic bag with a ½-inch opening cut from one corner.

Bake until evenly golden brown, 12 to 15 minutes, rotating the pans halfway through; a toothpick inserted into the center of the thickest part of one of the donuts should come out clean.

While the donuts bake, in a small bowl whisk the remaining ½ cup granulated sugar and 1 teaspoon cinnamon together. In a separate small bowl, melt the remaining 6 tablespoons butter in the microwave.

Let the donuts cool for 5 minutes after baking, then unmold them from the pans, brush with the melted butter, and dredge them in the cinnamon sugar while they are still warm.

Adapted from NYTimes.com's Erin Jeane McDowell.

Bud's "Special" Cannon Cove Brownies

Total Time: 5 hours
Makes 16 brownies

Making "special" brownies requires cannabutter, the key ingredient in cannabis edibles. Recipes for homemade cannabutter are plentiful online. Stoners have been making it for years, so how difficult can it be? If cannabis and its derivatives are not legal in your state, you can substitute regular unsalted butter in the same amount.

2 tablespoons unsalted butter, for greasing the pan
⅓ cup natural cocoa powder, plus a sprinkling for the pan
½ cup cannabutter
3 ounces dark chocolate, chopped
1 cup granulated sugar
1 tablespoon light corn syrup
1 teaspoon vanilla extract
¼ teaspoon salt
2 eggs
¾ cup all-purpose flour
½ cup chopped walnuts (optional)
¾ cup all-purpose flour

Preheat the oven to 350°F.

CONTINUED »

Grease an 8-inch square baking pan with the unsalted butter, and then dust with the cocoa powder. Set aside.

In a heatproof bowl over a pot of water set to simmer (or microwave in 10-second intervals), melt the cannabutter and chocolate. Remove the bowl from the heat. Add the sugar, corn syrup, vanilla, and salt.

Add the eggs one at a time, mixing well after each addition. Beat until a ribbon that lasts about 5 seconds forms on the top of the batter when you lift the whisk, about 5 minutes.

In a separate bowl, sift or whisk the flour with the cocoa powder, and then add it to the melted chocolate mixture. Stir just until the flour disappears (don't overmix). Stir in the chopped walnuts (if desired).

Pour the batter into the prepared pan and place it in the center of the oven and bake until a glossy top forms and starts to crack, about 25 minutes,

Let the brownies cool on a wire rack for at least 10 minutes before cutting.

Adapted from a recipe for Double-Chocolate Weed Brownies by Food52.com's Vanessa Lavorato.

Acknowledgments

Thank you to the real Bernie Sanders for the inspiration, and to the following authors whose books helped inform my fictional portrait of the senator: Jonathan Allen & Amie Parnes, W. J. Conroy, Greg Dawson, Heather Gautney, Huck Gutman, Harry Jaffe, Ari Rabin-Havt, Ted Rall, Chuck Rocha, Grant Stern, and Jonathan Tasini. To learn more about the real Bernie Sanders and his progressive agenda, get your head out of the sand and read the news—he's all over it.

Many thanks to Elizabeth Belchik for adding her special touch to the recipes and to Cheryl Redmond for her careful eye.

A deep debt of gratitude to the Vermonters (current and former) who put up with my pestering questions about the Green Mountain State and its quirks including Kira Gold. A special shout-out to the regional sugarmakers that assisted with my research. Alas, their contributions must remain on background due to the sensitive nature of the trade secrets they divulged. In keeping with the Vermont maple industry's strict code of secrecy, many of the sugaring tidbits and techniques within these pages have been heavily fictionalized.

Thank you to Matt Inman, Fariza Hawke, Ashley Pierce, Annie Marino, Mari Gill, Vi-An Nguyen, Dan Myers, David Hawk, Joseph Lozada, and Allison Renzulli at Ten Speed Press as well as Michael Fedison and Christine Jerome for bringing this book to life.

Thank you to Brandi Bowles and Mary Pender at UTA.

This book is dedicated to the memory of Stephanie Meyers—editor, writer, friend, mystery reader, Bears fan. She didn't write the Twilight books (you're thinking of Stephenie Meyer). She was, however, always happy to answer misdirected questions from Twilight fans on Twitter.

About The Author

Andrew Shaffer is the *New York Times* bestselling author of the Obama Biden mysteries *Hope Never Dies* and *Hope Rides Again*, the presidential satire *The Day of the Donald*, and more than a dozen other humorous works of genre fiction from mystery to horror. He is a flatlander who now calls Louisville, Kentucky, home. Shaffer and his wife, novelist Tiffany Reisz, recently welcomed a Cascade green Subaru Forester into their family.